Taking Chloe

The only way to keep what he has...is to surrender everything.

Merrick Vaughn couldn't be happier with his life. His business is jumping and his marriage to the love of his life is about as good as it gets. At least, that's what he thinks...until Chloe announces she wants to separate.

Stunned doesn't begin to cover it, but it quickly becomes clear that she's dead serious. And if he doesn't take action, as in now, he's going to lose the only woman he's ever loved.

The last thing Chloe wants is a divorce, but she can't go on living with a virtual stranger who spends all his time—and hers—behind a desk. It's tearing her apart, and taking a break to sort out her thoughts seems her only recourse.

Then Merrick offers a wicked proposition: go to Hawaii with him for one week's vacation. After that, if he hasn't successfully changed her mind, he'll let her go. No questions asked. There's only one caveat. She must agree to give him complete control.

Chloe's intrigued and scared. One week in paradise might bring them closer—or be their ultimate undoing.

Warning: This story contains graphic language, a touch of voyeurism, anal sex, and husband-and-wife lovin' in lots of sinful positions. Have your significant other handy!

Tempting Grace

A hard man is good to find...and impossible to resist.

Since a car accident left her unable to have children, Grace Vaughn has hidden her heart behind a wall. So far it's held strong, and no one complains much—except the few men she dates.

Now that fortress is crumbling thanks to Jackson Hill, an annoyingly attractive man who makes her imagination go wild just watching him in the office. He's practically bullied her into attending a Vegas conference with him. Three days alone with the delicious Jackson—in Sin City, no less—is sure to push her right over the edge.

With a loving family, a decent bank account, a nice set of clubs, Jackson's life is almost complete. Except for the missing piece. Grace. She sets a fire in his blood, and the conference is the perfect crowbar to get past her defense mechanisms. It's time to see if the bump-and-grind potential in that booty of hers can be channeled into something a little more satisfying than looking.

He's got just the tactic to get her to let down her guard—and hopefully her panties. A wicked bet. Because if there's one thing he knows about Grace, she can't resist a double-dog-dare...

Warning: This title contains graphic sex, rope bondage, anal sex, and a deliciously inventive hero who just happens to be really good with knots and doling out spankings.

Look for these titles by
Anne Rainey

Now Available:

Haley's Cabin
Burn
Turbulent Passions
Seduce Me

The Vaughn Series
Touching Lace (Book 1)
Tasting Candy (Book 2)
Taking Chloe (Book 3)
Tempting Grace (Book 4)

Coming Soon:

What She Wants

Dare Me

Anne Rainey

A SAMHAIN PUBLISHING, LTD. publication.

Samhain Publishing, Ltd.
577 Mulberry Street, Suite 1520
Macon, GA 31201
www.samhainpublishing.com

Dare Me
Print ISBN: 978-1-60504-781-2
Taking Chloe Copyright © 2010 by Anne Rainey
Tempting Grace Copyright © 2010 by Anne Rainey

Editing by Linda Ingmanson

Taking Chloe, ISBN 978-1-60504-575-7
First Samhain Publishing, Ltd. electronic publication: June 2009
Tempting Grace, ISBN 978-1-60504-655-6
First Samhain Publishing, Ltd. electronic publication: August 2009
First Samhain Publishing, Ltd. print publication: June 2010

Contents

Taking Chloe

Dedication

For my husband. You're the best thing that ever happened to me.

Chapter One

She couldn't have stopped the tears even if she'd wanted to. Seeing their honeymoon pictures had pushed her over the edge. They'd been so happy on the trip to Hawaii. Everything had felt right, blissful. Two years now and she still didn't understand how things had gone so wrong.

Chloe grabbed a tissue from the box next to the bed and dabbed at her eyes. Damn it, why couldn't she be stronger? Just smack Merrick upside his thick skull and force him to see what he was doing to their marriage? To her!

The eye-opener had come a month ago to the day. She'd woken up and rolled over and he'd been gone. At work on a Sunday morning. She'd known then that her life had slipped right on by and her husband was a ghost. A shell. She'd spent that awful day remembering every moment of the past two years and she'd come to a heartbreaking conclusion. She was married in name only.

Merrick's entire life revolved around his business. The success of Vaughn's Business Solutions mattered more than anything. She'd stupidly thought marriage would change him. Make him slow down. She'd been wearing some serious rose-colored glasses when she'd imagined them tying the knot and him working less. She'd had visions of the two of them spending more time enjoying life, enjoying each other. Maybe even talking about having kids. She'd deluded herself into believing she could sit him down and have a conversation, straighten things out. He'd listened, sure, but then he'd gotten a call on his cell and the discussion had come to an abrupt stop. He'd kissed her and promised to talk about it later. She'd waited and waited, but later never came.

A full thirty days later, here she sat, clutching her resume in her hand and wishing her husband would spend his Sunday with her instead of with client files. Chloe swiped at her eyes and threw the damp tissue across the room. It was time to take action. No way around it now.

She'd used the day to pack and cry. When Merrick had hurried out the door right after breakfast, she'd begun making plans. Hearing him explain that there were things that needed his immediate attention, swearing to come home early, had been the last straw. Enough already. The past several months had proved to be quite an eye opener. Merrick would never slow down. She'd had her wake up call, now it was time to get a backbone and deal with the prospect of spending the rest of her life without him.

Chloe stood and looked around the bedroom. Their bed, their dresser, their closet, she'd be leaving it all behind. And because she worked at his company, she'd be forced to get a new job as well. Unless by some miracle he'd come home and see what she was doing and talk her out of it.

"There you go again," she muttered. "Ever the optimist."

Chloe sighed and tucked the resume into her suitcase, then zipped it shut. She wheeled it out to the living room and placed it by the front door. Now all she had to do was sit and wait for Merrick.

She went to the refrigerator and poured a glass of water. Just as she brought it to her lips, she heard the squeaky motor of the automatic garage door. *Oh, God, I don't have the strength!*

The firm bang of Merrick's car door had her heart beating erratically. Chloe set her glass on the counter and watched, waited.

Merrick slipped quietly into the kitchen, exhausted as always, a frown marring his handsome features. He caught sight of her and smiled. "Hey, babe," he whispered as he kissed her on the cheek, "you didn't have to wait up."

Her stomach fluttered. "I wanted to talk to you about something."

He pushed a hand through his shiny dark hair. "Sure, let's talk in bed, though, I'm beat."

She knew that tone. As soon as his head hit the pillow, he'd be out like a light. She could forget about a conversation after that because he wouldn't remember any of it in the morning.

"I'd rather talk now, Merrick."

Merrick took a sip of her water before patting her on the back. "Okay, just let me go change out of this monkey suit."

Chloe sighed. "Sure."

After waiting a full ten minutes, she searched him out. It was no surprise to find him sprawled across the bed in his boxers, sound asleep. Tears sprang to her eyes. Grabbing the throw blanket at the end of the bed, she covered him up before turning out the light. She walked softly to the office and picked up a pen and notepad from the desk, then scrawled out a note. She took it to the kitchen and placed it in front of the coffee pot where he'd be sure to see it in the morning.

As she took her keys off the hook by the door, Chloe allowed herself one last wistful look around the house. It felt empty, lonely. In the beginning, they'd made love on nearly every surface. They'd laughed in the kitchen as they'd debated who was the worst cook. They'd chatted about silly things and argued over which movie to watch on Friday nights. Now, nothing. Just a house and a man who'd given his soul to his job.

Chloe closed the door and locked it, then got in her car and drove slowly down the street. This time the tears didn't come. Sadness and an overwhelming sense of finality filled her. Once Merrick saw the note, there'd be a talk, but in the end he'd choose his job. He always did.

♦

"You really did it? You're sitting in a hotel right now alone?"

"Yeah," Chloe mumbled. "I just couldn't take another second, Lace. I can't sit around and watch him work himself into an early grave. I just can't do it."

"I understand, but I wish you would've come here. Nick's house is plenty big enough, sweetie."

So she could watch the two of them hold each other and kiss and do all the romantic things she wished Merrick would do with her? She loved Lacey like a sister, but there was no way she could handle seeing that type of love right now. "No, I don't want to intrude. I'll be fine here for now."

"Okay, but have you considered who you're dealing with here?"

"What do you mean?" Chloe held the phone between her shoulder and ear and clutched at the pillow. It wasn't Merrick's pillow. She couldn't smell his scent. Her stomach suddenly felt hollow. Oh, God, she already missed him.

"I know my brother. He won't just let you walk away. That's not how this is going to play out. You know that, right?"

Lacey saw her brother in a different light. She couldn't really blame Lacey, either. Chloe had no siblings, but she could understand that type of relationship. One of the things she loved about the Vaughns was how close they all were. A divorce would mean leaving them all behind, not just Merrick. It made her sick just thinking about it.

Unlike the large, close-knit Vaughn family, Chloe had only her father now that her mother was gone, and they weren't at all close. He kept to his work as a financial advisor and they talked a few times a month. She'd never wished for more because she'd had her mother to fill the void. After ovarian cancer had taken her from them five years ago, Chloe had grieved the loss of not only her mother, but her best friend. Chloe had never dreamed she'd marry into such a rowdy, loving bunch as the Vaughns. She'd been so blessed to have a mother-in-law as open and accepting as Marie. The thought of losing not only Merrick, but his family as well...it was simply too much to contemplate.

"Chloe?"

Chloe snapped back to the here and now. "I don't think you realize how dedicated your brother is to the business. He's become obsessed, Lace. I can't get through to him."

Chloe heard a shuffling sound, then a male voice in the background. Lacey's fiancé Nick. They'd been engaged for a while, driving the family crazy by not setting a date for the wedding. Nick was so in love with Lacey. It was sweet and beautiful, but sometimes Chloe felt a pang of jealousy for Merrick's baby sister. After all, Lacey had a man who loved her and spent time with her.

"He's become a workaholic, I know," Lacey agreed. "But I also know how much he loves you. It took the dunce awhile to realize he cared about you as more than a good worker and a friend. Once he admitted to himself that you were the woman for him there was no going back. He's not going to let you walk off into the sunset, not without him right beside you, anyway."

Frustration started to set in as she listened to Lacey's gentle words. "I didn't want any of this either. When he proposed, I thought it was for life. I'm the happy-ever-after kind of woman. My parents were so happy before Mom died. I think if cancer hadn't taken her, they'd still be spending endless amounts of time together." She took a breath, then said, "But living with Merrick has become impossible. He works constantly. Lacey, he's well beyond reasoning. I tried! What am I supposed to do? Sit around and hope he comes to his senses?"

"Of course not, that's not what I meant. Heck, I'm proud of you for sticking to your guns. Merrick didn't marry a spineless wuss. He married an intelligent woman with a backbone. But you need to understand he isn't exactly the silent type. He'll come to his senses damn quick. When he does, he's going to do everything in his power to get you back. You've seen how hard he's worked to make Vaughn's Business Solutions a success. He pours every ounce of himself into a project. When he wakes up and realizes you've moved out, he's going to get angry at first, then he'll start thinking, planning. He loves you, and a man in love can be very creative when he sets his mind to it. I should know."

"You're beginning to scare me." Merrick would never hurt her, but he would attempt to break down her defenses. Lacey was right about that.

"Merrick's a very driven man. The question is, how hard do you want to fight and how far are you willing to run before you let him catch you?"

That piqued her ire. "This isn't a game. This isn't a stunt to gain his attention. This is the real thing."

She heard Lacey laugh. "I hear you, but I also know how much you love my annoying, pigheaded, sometimes blind brother. And I don't think you're quite ready to contemplate divorce."

"I saw an attorney."

"Yeah, you saw an attorney. And?"

Chloe gritted her teeth. Score one for Lacey. Chloe had visited with an attorney, but she hadn't gone back. After the initial consultation, Chloe had gone to work in tears. When Merrick had caught her at her desk, dabbing at her eyes, she'd told him it was PMS. He'd let it go.

"You're right. I'm not ready for a divorce. But Merrick isn't leaving me much choice, is he? And I updated my resume, too. I'll have to find another job, a new place to live."

"We'll see."

For the first time in days, Chloe felt a measure of hope. Maybe all wasn't lost. Maybe Merrick would come to his senses. If it was one thing she knew about Merrick Vaughn, the man could be as tenacious as a pit bull. Dangling fresh meat in front of him could prove seriously dangerous.

Chapter Two

Merrick woke with a start. His eyes popped open and he had a sudden need to finish something important, but he couldn't remember what the hell he'd left undone. He ran a hand through his hair and groaned. "Damn, I'm losing my mind."

He closed his eyes again and slid his palm across the bed, expecting to encounter the soft, supple skin of his wife. Nothing. He opened his eyes and turned his head. He rubbed his eyes and looked again. *Chloe's up?* She never got up before him.

Merrick left the bed and washed up in the adjoining bathroom, then went searching for his wife. He checked the office first, figuring maybe she'd decided to get an early start, but there was no sign of her. He rubbed his stomach and made his way to the kitchen. With any luck, she was already getting the coffee started, but it was empty, too. His gaze snagged on a piece of paper in front of the coffee pot. He strode across the room and picked it up.

Merrick,

I'm sorry to leave with no warning, but you gave me no choice. I've tried so many times to talk to you, but you're always too busy with work. I appreciate your need to make a success of yourself, but it's killing me to watch our marriage go down the drain. I didn't come by this decision easily. I love you, I always will, but I think we need some time apart.

I'm staying at a hotel in town. Call my cell when you get this, we'll talk.

Love always,

Chloe

Merrick read the note three times. "What the hell?" he grumbled as he reached for the cordless. He dialed, but it took him two tries to get the number right, his hands shook too damn bad.

"Hello?"

"Where are you?" he demanded.

"Merrick?"

He rolled his eyes. "Who else would be calling at six in the morning?"

"The connection is bad. I'll call you back on the hotel phone."

"Fine," he gritted out. He ended the call and waited. A hotel room? Was there another man with her? Merrick's rage boiled over at the images rolling through his mind. As the phone rang, he snatched it up. "Where the hell are you?"

"Don't yell at me, Merrick."

He knew that stubborn tone. He'd get nowhere if he came at her like an angry steer. "Tell me what's going on, babe."

"I tried to tell you last night, but you were too tired, as usual. Did you even notice that my bags were packed?"

"I was damned exhausted, Chloe," he snarled. "I didn't take an inventory of the house."

"Yeah, I noticed. How about my car? Didn't you wonder why it was in the driveway instead of the garage the way it usually is?"

Merrick hadn't even seen her car. He'd driven home by rote. He even suspected he'd closed his eyes for a few seconds too long during the drive. None of that mattered now. All that mattered was getting Chloe home, where she damn well belonged. "Come home so we can talk about this," he urged.

"No. If I come home we won't talk. Besides, you need to get ready for work. By the way, I'm taking the day off."

"Damn it, Chloe. What's going on?"

"We'll meet for lunch."

It was better than chatting on the damn phone like strangers. "Fine. Where?"

"Sal's."

Chloe's favorite Italian restaurant. "I'll be there at noon," he agreed.

"Okay, and Merrick?"

"Yeah?"

"This isn't about another man. I...I just wanted you to know that."

Merrick let out a sigh of relief. "Whatever it is, babe, we can deal with it together."

"I don't know. I just don't."

Merrick hated hearing the defeat in his wife's voice. "I love you, Chloe. That'll never change."

"I know. I love you, too."

They ended the call and he stood in the center of the kitchen, chilled to the bone. How had everything gone to hell without him even realizing it? Why hadn't he seen it coming?

His mind rebelled at the notion that she might not come back. He refused to believe that. He'd envisioned her pregnant with his baby some day. There would be no other, not for him. Chloe was the only woman he ever loved. She *would* be back in his arms. In his bed.

He looked at the clock on the wall. Any other day he'd be in his car on his way to work by now. His mind would be on the meetings scheduled throughout the day and the clients he needed to finesse. Today, all his thoughts centered on the sadness in Chloe's voice. Had he brought that on? His gut tightened as he read the note again. The words *busy with work* jumped out at him. He had been working a lot lately, more so than usual. But having a wife and contemplating a baby had made him think of the future. Specifically, providing for his family and making it so they would want for nothing. He'd had an overwhelming need to give them a life of comfort. Chloe deserved the best and he couldn't give her that unless he made Vaughn's Business Solutions a success.

A little voice inside him mocked him for a liar. The business was already a success. He worked himself to death *why*? He studiously ignored the annoying question and started working on the current problem. He'd meet Chloe at noon and, no matter what, he'd bring his wife home.

Merrick grabbed the phone and dialed information, then called the florist and ordered eighteen long stem roses. Once that was finished, he called his office.

"Vaughn's Business Solutions, Candice speaking, may I help you?"

"Candice, it's Merrick. I'm taking the day off. I need you to cancel all my appointments for the day."

He heard Candice giggle. "Chloe just called in sick, too. You two playing hooky?"

Merrick felt a muscle in his jaw jump in frustration. "No, nothing like that. We just need a day off."

21

"You've been working around the clock. You deserve a break. I'll take care of everything. Have fun."

Fun? When was the last time he'd had fun? "Thanks, sweetheart." As they were about to hang up, he thought of something else. "Hey, have you talked to Blade today?"

"Yeah, he's at home. He's working on a bid for that big strip mall."

"Thanks, talk to you later."

"Merrick, if you see Blade, tell him to call me. I need him to pick up some things from the store."

Merrick laughed. His brother Blade and Candice had started dating about the same time he'd married Chloe. Now they were happily married themselves and talking about kids. "My brother grocery shopping? That's so messed up."

Candice's laughter filled his ear. "I aim to domesticate that Neanderthal if it's the last thing I do."

Merrick snorted. "Good luck with that."

"Are you saying he's beyond help?"

"I'm saying I know my brother. You'll never housebreak him, but watching you try has been damned interesting."

Candice made a tsking sound. "You should have more faith in him. He's done very well since we tied the knot. He even cooks dinner a few nights a week."

That shocked him. "Really?"

"Well," she hedged, "I admit it's only macaroni and cheese and frozen dinners, but it's a start."

"Candice, if anyone can bring that man a measure of civility it's you."

"Thanks."

"No, on behalf of the Vaughn family, thank *you* for bringing

Blade into the twenty-first century."

They said their goodbyes and ended the call. Merrick went to the bedroom and pulled a pair of jeans out of the dresser drawer, then grabbed the black t-shirt he'd flung over the back of a chair the day before. While he dressed, he started making a mental list. Get advice from Blade. Pick up flowers. Coax his wife into giving him a second chance. Jesus, he was pathetic. For a man with a master's degree in business and a million-dollar company, he sure didn't have much of an imagination. He needed to figure out why Chloe felt their relationship was beyond repair. He'd need to convince her that working things out would be the best route. The only problem with that plan? Chloe's stubbornness. Once she made a decision, there'd be no changing her mind. He loved her decisiveness and goal-oriented attitude, but at times that trait could prove annoying as hell.

As he slipped into his work boots and grabbed his keys, he glanced around the living room. His chest ached. There were signs of Chloe everywhere, in the mauve couches she'd picked out and the matching wall hangings. The fluffy rug in front of the fireplace had been her idea, too. She'd claimed it would prove romantic. As he stared at it, he realized he couldn't remember the last time they'd spent time together on it. He'd been burning the candle at both ends; as a result, his marriage had suffered. What a joke. He'd worked to give them a better life, but he'd been too damn busy to enjoy the life he already had.

Merrick closed the door and locked it, determination settling into every fiber of his being. The next time he looked at the damn fireplace, it'd be from the floor, with Chloe naked and riding his cock and taking them both to heaven.

◆

"You and Chloe separated?"

"Temporarily," he reiterated for the third time. "It's not a permanent situation."

"Yeah," Blade said as he went to the fridge. "Want a beer?"

Merrick frowned. "I thought Candice didn't like alcohol in the house."

Blade shrugged and grabbed two light beers, then handed one to him. "Candy knows I'm not a big drinker, so she doesn't mind."

Four years ago, a man she worked with had raped Candice. The bastard had slipped something into her drink. Since then she never touched alcohol. After she'd met Blade, everything changed, for the better. It thrilled Merrick to see her so happy. The difference in her attitude and appearance had been nothing short of miraculous.

Merrick twisted off the cap and took a long swig, then sat at the kitchen table. "I don't know what the hell happened. One minute I'm a happily married man, the next I'm waking up to an empty house. How is that even possible?"

"You want the truth?"

"Yes," Merrick answered as he squared his shoulders for the assault that would surely come. Blade was all about confronting an issue head on.

"She got tired of being a widow."

Merrick slammed his beer down on the table. "What the hell is that supposed to mean?"

"It means you spend more time at that office than you do with her. You work nearly twenty-four hours a day and you never take weekends off. That wears on a woman, Merrick."

"I've been trying to make things better for her. I'd like to have kids someday and I think Chloe would like to be a stay-at-home mom. She's talked about it more than once. But, that won't happen if I can't get the business where it needs to be."

"Bullshit."

Merrick rolled his eyes. "Why not tell me how you really feel, Blade?"

"That business of yours isn't exactly paltry, and you know it. What's really holding you back?"

Merrick clenched his fist around the bottle. "I don't know what you mean."

"Are you afraid?"

"Damn it, Blade!"

Blade held up a hand. "Just hear me out." He paused, and Merrick nodded. "If you ask me, I think you're afraid of not measuring up. Not being the husband Chloe needs, not being the father you imagine. I think it scares the shit out of you every time you think about the future."

Merrick didn't know what to say. He'd never let himself think too hard about his insecurities. Men just weren't wired that way. Having Blade throw it in his face made it real. He had been afraid. Terrified, actually. "Chloe is my whole world. I keep thinking she's going to wake up and wonder why she married my dumb ass."

Blade smiled. "Yeah, we all think that way. But burying your head in the sand isn't the answer."

"Gee, you think?"

"Smartass," Blade grumbled.

"Dickhead," Merrick shot right back.

They both took a swig of their beers. Blade stood and tossed the bottle in the trash. He crossed his arms over his chest and said, "So, what are you going to do about it? Sit on

25

your ass and bitch like a little girl, or get your woman back?"

Merrick stood and pinned Blade with a hard glare. "Get my woman back."

"Good answer. Now, it seems to me you need to get her away. Take her some place where it's just the two of you. No job, no interruptions."

Merrick thought of the last time he'd taken Chloe away. "Hawaii," he uttered.

"A second honeymoon? Yep, that should do the trick."

Blade was so sure, but he hadn't heard the stubbornness in Chloe's voice that morning. "What if it doesn't? What if she still wants a divorce?"

"Then you tie her cute ass to the bed and keep her there."

Merrick laughed and shook his head. "Oh, yeah, you're all reformed."

Blade frowned. "Huh?"

"Never mind," he said as he made his way to the door. "Just tell Candice that I said she's got a lot more work to do."

As Merrick left the house, got into his car and started the engine, a plan began to form. Hawaii. Yeah, he'd take her to Hawaii, but it wouldn't be like their honeymoon. Back then he'd been content to let things flow. He'd been hopelessly in love, not a care in the world. This time around, he'd be fighting for his life, his future.

Chapter Three

Chloe sat at their usual table in the back of Sal's restaurant. Sal, the owner, came over and took her hand in his. "You're as beautiful as ever, darling."

She winked and said, "And you're a shameless flirt, Sal, as always."

"Where's that man of yours?"

"He's on his way. He should be here any minute." A voice in the back of her mind taunted her with the notion that he may not show at all. That he'd gotten lost in his work. Again.

"His loss is my gain, pretty Chloe," Sal murmured, then kissed the back of her hand.

Chloe laughed. "Do you treat all your lady customers this way?"

He took a step backward and said, "Of course!"

"I think maybe you shouldn't be hitting on my woman."

The gruff male voice had Chloe sitting up straighter and clutching her purse in her lap. Merrick. And he wasn't wearing a suit. Hadn't he gone to work? She let her gaze travel over him, taking in the tight, faded jeans and black t-shirt. His dark tousled hair looked as if he hadn't even bothered to run a comb through it. Still he was the most handsome man she'd ever seen.

"I'd never dream of it, boy. Just keeping her company until you got here."

Merrick's eyebrow shot up. "You're a bad liar, Sal."

Sal smacked Merrick on the back. "You're just jealous because she likes me better."

Chloe wanted to laugh, but held back. Sal was in his midsixties. Not only had he been happily married for forty years, but he also had six kids and thirteen grandkids.

"That flirting is going to get you in a world of trouble one of these days."

"So my wife keeps telling me," he admitted. As Merrick came closer, Sal asked, "The usual?"

Their usual was spaghetti and meatballs with a bottle of merlot, then chocolate cake for dessert. They always shared the cake and stuffed themselves. Today, Chloe didn't feel like eating at all.

"Sounds great. Thanks," Merrick answered for them both.

After Sal shuffled off, Merrick brought his right arm around from behind his back, revealing a long box. Flowers? He'd bought her flowers *and* taken the day off work?

Merrick set the box on the table in front of her. She stared at it as if it were a snake. It'd been so long since Merrick had bought her flowers.

"Open it, babe."

Chloe looked up at him. The hurt in his eyes was plain to see. Her heart broke. She reached out and tugged the box closer, then slowly opened it. A beautiful bouquet of long stem roses. "They're lovely," she whispered, her voice shaking. "Thank you."

Merrick reached his hand out to hers. Chloe let him twine their fingers together. "What's going on, babe? Why'd you leave me?"

Chloe heard the pain in her husband's deep, low voice, and she ached to put them both out of their misery, but she couldn't give in to her heart's desire. If she caved now, he'd be right back to his old ways, and she'd be no better off than she was now. She shored up her nerve. If she made it through the next few hours without falling apart, it'd be a miracle.

"A separation," she answered without preamble. "I don't know if there will be more to it than that, but I need some time to think."

Merrick tightened his hold on her hand and gritted out, "Yeah, I got that much from the note, but that doesn't give me a why. Please make me understand why my wife saw fit to leave me while I was asleep. Explain how that's any kind of solution to whatever's wrong with our marriage, Chloe."

She wiggled her fingers and he loosened his hold, but didn't pull away. She hadn't really expected him to. This was Merrick at his most dominating. He would never give up without a fight. She'd known that, but she also knew that once he realized he'd have to choose between his back-to-back work schedule and her, he'd choose his work.

"It's not as if I woke up yesterday and decided to walk out on everything I've worked so hard to build. This has been building for a long time. I've tried to talk to you, to make you slow down. You work fourteen-hour days, Merrick. Your entire world revolves around the business. At first I admired your drive. Now I realize it's not drive, it's an obsession. You spend all your waking hours at that office. Since I work there, too, I do get to see you, but it's not the same as spending time together as husband and wife, and you know it. I spend every weekend alone. Do you know how that makes me feel? Have you any idea how sick I am of being second to that damned business?"

Merrick frowned. "You were never second, sweetheart."

Chloe saw red. "You can sit there and say that to me? You're a liar, Merrick Vaughn."

He made a shushing sound. "Keep your voice down unless you want everyone to know our personal problems."

She took a deep breath and tried to calm her racing heart. A waiter brought their wine and poured a small amount in each of their glasses, then shuffled off to another table. Chloe took a sip, then sat back and waited for him to continue.

Merrick's gaze never left her face. He didn't acknowledge the waiter or the wine. His anger and hurt were evident in the set of his shoulders and the jumping muscle in his jaw. Chloe desperately wanted to soothe him. Tell him it was all a mistake. But that path wasn't going to bring her happiness, only more grief.

"You never said anything," he said finally. "I had no idea you were this unhappy. Why, Chloe?"

She slumped in her seat. "I tried talking to you, several times. You would either promise to be home more, which never happened, or you'd wave my concerns away as if I were suffering from a particularly vicious bout of PMS or something. After awhile, I stopped trying."

Merrick was quiet for a long time. Chloe couldn't tell what he was thinking. Sal brought their food and chatted with them a moment then left them to eat in privacy. She wanted to shove her plate away. Just the thought of eating the rich sauce and savory meatballs made her stomach queasy, but it was better than sitting in total silence.

Merrick released her hand and they both ate several bites before giving up. She peeked at Merrick and watched as he swiped a napkin over his mouth. That small gesture was sexier than a room full of exotic male dancers to Chloe. How could she possibly get over the man when she melted every time they were in the same room together?

When he sat back and crossed his arms over his chest, Chloe shivered. She recognized the determination in his dark blue eyes. Merrick was gearing up for a battle. He'd gotten the same look in meetings over the years. That look said, *I'm going to win and there's nothing you can do about it.*

"I have a proposition for you," Merrick said, his voice a low rumble that skated over her nerve endings like a hot caress.

"Okay, I'm listening." She couldn't even begin to guess at what Merrick had in mind.

"I want to take you on vacation. An entire week, just the two of us."

"That won't solve our problems. I wish that was all it would take, but the instant we come back, you'll be back to working around the clock and I'll be right back to waiting for you to remember that you're married."

Merrick's gaze never changed, but she could see that her words affected him. His entire body tensed. "I didn't forget we were married, but I see I've neglected you. I know I've been a lousy husband lately, but I think I deserve a chance to make it up to you. To make you see that I can change. That I *will* change."

She badly wanted to believe him. She needed to believe him, and that scared her more than anything. He was her life, her only love. Divorce wouldn't change how her heart felt. She would always belong to Merrick. Still, she needed to protect her heart from more pain.

"I don't know, Merrick. I've tried so many times to get you to hear me, but nothing ever worked."

"I was a blind fool. I know that now. When I read your note and realized you'd left me, I felt like my entire life had come to a

31

screeching halt. I'm asking you to give me a chance to save our marriage. Let me have a week alone with you. If you're still determined that a separation is the only answer, then I'll let you go, no questions."

"One week?" she asked, hesitant but for the first time hopeful.

Merrick nodded. "One week alone. No work, not even via the computer. It'll be all about you and me, baby."

She liked the sound of that, and he knew it. Damn it. "Where?"

"Hawaii."

Oh, God, a second honeymoon. Merrick was much better at playing emotional warfare than she'd ever imagined. But as she well knew, words were one thing, actually putting plan to action was all together different.

"You can't just take off. I'm your administrative assistant, remember? Your calendar is full. Leaving the business for a full week is out of the question."

"I took today off and the place didn't burn down. I reckon a week won't hurt either. Besides, Jackson is more than capable of stepping in. We both know it. Stop making excuses."

He was right. Jackson, his Vice President of Operations, was fully capable of handling things. It might very well prove to be the biggest mistake of her life if she went away with Merrick now. She might end up hurting even more. Could she possibly turn down this last ditch effort to save their marriage, though? She loved him too much not to try one more time.

"Okay."

Merrick's smile wasn't at all comforting. "There's one catch."

Well, of course there was! She should've seen that one

coming a mile away. A man didn't build a million-dollar company from the ground up and not have a few tricks up his sleeve.

"What are you thinking?" she ground out. "Out with it."

"You do everything I say. I'm in charge of our fun in and out of the bedroom while we're there."

She quirked a brow at his choice of words. "Our fun?"

"You do as I say. Exactly as I say. You'll turn yourself over to me completely." He leaned close as he murmured, "The last day is yours to do with as you wish. You can order me to suck your toes if you want and I'll do it. I'll be putty in your hands, baby."

The idea was way more appealing than it should've been. "You've never let me do that. You like to have control."

"And you usually like me in control. But this is a special occasion. Besides, I don't think it'll be too much of a hardship."

"Are you certain you won't get cold feet?"

He uncrossed his arms and leaned forward, dark promise in his heated gaze. "Try me, baby."

Chloe's pussy flooded with liquid warmth.

Chapter Four

Merrick shifted in his seat as he watched the hotel Chloe had run off to. He'd been watching over her since they'd left Sal's. His instinct was to charge in there. He could easily rip the door off its hinges, toss her over his shoulder and bring her ass home. That would be the easy thing to do. The barbaric thing. Instead, he gave her the space she needed and silently kept watch, making sure she stayed safe. Hell, it wasn't like he was going to get any sleep without her anyway. He might as well stand guard.

In the restaurant, she'd looked so pretty sitting at the table with her long, dark hair hanging past her shoulders in soft waves. The pink blouse she'd worn hadn't been able to hide her full, round breasts, either. Chloe's curvy body never failed to stir his libido, but the sadness in her eyes had stopped him cold. He wanted that look gone.

His cell beeped, dragging him away from thoughts of Chloe alone in a cold hotel bed. Merrick grabbed it off the middle console and flipped it open. "Yeah," he grumbled.

"You're not still there. Tell me you're at home."

It was the third time Blade had called to check up on him, as if he were a snot nosed kid. "I can't leave her alone," he explained yet again, barely holding onto his temper. "She's never been alone. Even before we met she had a roommate."

"It's a nice hotel, bro. Hell, she's not staying in some fleabag in the south end. She'll be fine. You need to get some sleep."

"Not without Chloe," he reaffirmed. "I'm not getting back into that bed without my wife tucked in beside me."

He heard Blade sigh, then mumble something, probably to Candice. "We'll come and take over guard duty," he announced, as if it were a done deal. "Candice is worried and it's pissing me off. You need to go home and get some rest, and I want my wife to stop worrying, damn it."

He hated this. At three in the morning, Blade and Candice should be sound asleep. Instead they were awake and stressing over his dumb ass. "Look, I appreciate the offer, but I wouldn't sleep anyway. I'm fine, okay?"

"Tell that to Candy," he snarled.

Merrick heard what sounded like sheets ruffling around, then Candice's soft voice filled his ear. "Merrick, I wish you would try and get some rest. Blade and I don't mind coming over to watch out for Chloe. Really."

Merrick pushed a hand through his hair, wishing like hell he'd never let his life get so twisted up. "Candice, I love you for offering. I just can't leave her. If sitting in this car, watching her window is all I can have of my wife right now, then I'm going to take it. Does that make sense?"

"Of course it does," she said softly. "If you need us for anything, please don't hesitate to call."

God, he had a great family. He didn't know if he deserved them, but he was damn lucky to have their love and support. "Thanks, hon. Get some rest now, or else Blade's going to kick my ass."

Candice laughed. "He wouldn't dare. He's much too gentle."

Merrick nearly choked. "Gentle?"

"You heard the woman. I'm as gentle as a lamb."

"Right, you and Genghis Khan."

"Damn straight. Anyway, like Candy girl said, you need us, call."

"Will do. Thanks, Blade."

They said their goodbyes and hung up. Merrick moved the seat back and stretched out. In his mind, he kept hearing the dejection in Chloe's voice as she told him she was tired of playing second fiddle to his work. The company didn't mean more to him than she did, but he couldn't really blame her for coming to that conclusion.

Changing the situation wouldn't be easy. He didn't just work at Vaughn's Business Solutions, he owned the damn place. He did work fourteen-hour days and he had been spending his weekends at the office just as Chloe claimed. The insane schedule had become routine. The only way to fix it would be to delegate some of the responsibility. He needed to lessen his load so he could spend more time being a husband. He would work it out, no matter what. Chloe was his world.

Damn, it was going to be a long night.

♦

It'd taken three days to wrap up everything at the office and rearrange his and Chloe's schedules. In her capacity as his Administrative Assistant, Chloe saw to it that his meetings were either rescheduled or handled by Jackson. At the end of the third day, Candice had ushered them both out of the office with orders to have fun and relax. Merrick had made the plane reservations and called the hotel to reserve a suite. Their bags were packed. The only thing left was the drive to the airport.

Lacey called and announced she'd be dropping them at the airport. She'd claimed it wouldn't be safe to leave their car at the airport for a week. Merrick knew she had a point, but he also knew Lacey wanted to give Chloe a pep talk. The drive was only a means to an end.

"If I'd known what a crazy driver you were, sis, I never would have let you take us." Merrick scowled as Lacey took the curve too fast and pulled into the airport lot.

"You're welcome," Lacey grumbled as she pulled up to the curb at the drop-off spot.

Merrick smiled and flung open the car door, then moved to retrieve their luggage from the trunk. He could hear murmurs from inside the car. He wondered for a minute what Lacey was saying. He shuddered. Hell, it was better not to know. When he noticed Chloe hugging his sister and leaving the car, he breathed a sigh of relief.

As she came around to the back to help him with the luggage, Merrick said, "I've got these."

When she tried to grab one of the heavier suitcases, Merrick handed her the shoulder bag instead. Chloe didn't argue. In fact, she wasn't saying much of anything. Was she nervous about the trip? Christ knew he shook like a damn leaf in a fall breeze. You'd think they hadn't been married for the last two years, the way his heart pounded and his palms sweated. He was fighting for his life here, though. She was giving him a shot to prove himself. If he screwed it up, she'd leave and there'd be no changing her mind. Fuck, no pressure there!

♦

Several hours later, Merrick's hopes were steadily falling. The plane trip had been annoying as hell. Chloe either sat quietly and read a magazine or slept. Her subdued attitude worried him. Any time he tried to draw her into a conversation, she'd talk in short sentences, never saying more than necessary. He'd really made a mess of things.

He had a solution though; at least he hoped he had a solution. After sleeping in his car outside her hotel two nights in a row—he still had an annoying crick in his neck—he'd finally come onto a plan. The alone time had allowed him a chance to work out a way to relieve himself of some of his duties so he could spend less time at work. The way he saw it, the biggest problem was all the social events he attended after hours. They were necessary, but majorly time consuming. When he returned from their trip, Merrick would need to talk to Jackson to find out if he'd be willing to take them on. For now, he only wanted to concentrate on rekindling the spark in his marriage. He only hoped he hadn't missed his chance.

Chloe had always pushed him to his limits. Since the first day she came to work for him, she'd stretched the walls of his comfort zone. She had a quiet way about her that made him want to just sit and watch her. She drifted around his office as if on air, getting things done with a slow but steady pace. He'd noticed her efficiency, then he'd noticed her curves. Chloe was the type of woman a man would kill to possess. Every man in his company had drooled over her the instant she'd glided through the doors. She made a man want to sit up and beg. Her smiles alone made him want to drop down on all fours and pant like a damn dog in heat.

After a few months of denying their mutual attraction, Merrick had asked her out to dinner. He'd gleefully broken one of his own cardinal rules: never get involved with an employee.

Halfway through the filet mignon, he'd figured out there'd be no ignoring the chemistry arcing back and forth. A dinner invitation had turned into an entire weekend spent in bed together. Merrick hadn't fought, he'd dived head first into love after that. It'd felt right when he'd proposed marriage. As corny as it seemed, he'd known deep down in his soul Chloe was his other half.

Now, as they sat side by side in the taxi heading to the hotel, a new determination rose up. He'd win his wife back, one way or the other. She was the only woman he would ever love. There would be no divorce. No splitting up the pans and towels. If he had anything to do with it, Chloe would be his again, inside and out.

As they arrived at the hotel, the same one they'd stayed in for their honeymoon, he heard Chloe gasp.

He reached across the seat and took her hand in his. It was so automatic; Merrick hadn't even thought to stop himself from comforting her. As she clutched onto him, he let go the tension that had dogged him during the plane trip. "Are you okay, baby?"

"I can't believe we're really here."

The breathless voice and small note of surprise seemed like a good sign, and Merrick wanted to hold onto it with all his strength. "Believe it. I aim to pamper and pleasure you this week. Nothing negative from this moment forward, agreed?"

Chloe looked over at him for the first time since they'd arrived in Honolulu, her eyes bright with unshed tears. "Agreed."

Now they were getting somewhere. He could practically see the walls coming down. Or at least cracking a little around the edges. By the end of the trip, he'd have her, body and soul, and she'd have him.

If he didn't screw it up.

After he paid the driver, Merrick opened the door and stepped out, then reached in to help Chloe. She took it without hesitation. When she emerged from the dark interior, Merrick had to stifle the urge to kiss her. She was so beautiful. Her long, straight, dark hair shone in the Hawaiian sun. The red t-shirt and blue jeans she'd worn for the long plane ride lovingly cupped her curves. How long had it been since he'd made love to his wife? Jesus, he couldn't even remember. He'd been such an ass! It was no wonder she'd left him. Chloe wasn't about to be a doormat, and that's exactly how he'd treated her. Some women might put up with being second fiddle, but his Chloe had too much self-respect. Merrick was ashamed he'd put her in the position of having to choose between their marriage and her happiness. They should be one and the same.

"It hasn't changed," Chloe murmured. "Not one bit."

"No," Merrick agreed as he watched her face light up with delight. "Still as beautiful as ever."

Chloe's gaze rested on his. He was surprised to see her cheeks turn pink with embarrassment. God, it was like their honeymoon all over again. This had been a good idea, no doubt about it.

"Come on," he urged as he placed his palm at the small of her back, "let's get checked in, then we can shower and go out for some dinner. Remember that little restaurant we'd found the first time we came here? The one with the open fire pit? I thought we'd go there tonight. You liked their lobster, right?"

"Yes, it was heavenly. I can't believe you remember that."

As the bellhop gathered their suitcases and loaded them onto the trolley, Merrick turned to Chloe and whispered into her ear, "I remember everything, baby."

"Do you?"

He cupped her chin and said, "I might've had a moment of stupidity, but you've got my attention now. I plan to spend the week showing you just what I remember. Who knows, maybe we'll even manage to make a few new memories."

"I'm afraid," Chloe admitted.

That surprised him. "Of me?"

She shook her head and looked away.

"Then what?" When she held back, he prompted further. "You can tell me."

Her gaze held a wealth of pain when she looked at him again. "It was hard to make the decision to separate. It's not something I wanted and I'm afraid of being hurt again. Of being vulnerable to you, Merrick."

He understood that feeling well. Still, how could he have made her so unhappy? Why hadn't he seen it? He'd been so damn selfish. Merrick cradled her face in his palms and murmured, "I will not disappoint you. Never again, baby. As God is my witness I'll do everything in my power to prove myself to you."

For long seconds Chloe simply stared at him, then she softly said, "I never needed you to prove anything to me. I love you, and that hasn't changed. I only need you to be my husband."

Merrick leaned down and kissed her, light and teasing, then whispered against her lips, "By the end of the week, you'll see that I'm still and will always be your husband." Chloe started to speak, but Merrick stopped her with a finger to her lips. "We're gathering an audience."

She looked around. When she noticed several people staring, her eyes grew as round as quarters.

"Come on," he urged, as he dropped his hand. "Let's check

in and see about dinner."

Chloe started forward, the sway of her hips capturing his attention. It seemed as natural as breathing to let his hand drift a little lower, just barely grazing the top of her ass. When he caressed her there, she missed a step and stumbled. Merrick caught her before she could fall forward.

"Merrick," she chastised.

"Just a little reminder."

"Of what?"

"That you're mine."

Chloe's spine stiffened, but she didn't deny his words. They went to the check-in desk and retrieved their room keys. On the ride up in the elevator, she talked to the bellhop about his job, the weather, the lovely hotel, and completely avoided her husband altogether. Merrick was on edge. When he caught sight of the youth checking out Chloe, his blood started to boil. If he looked at her tits one more time, Merrick would gladly wipe the lecherous grin right off his face. With his fist.

As Merrick glanced at Chloe, he could see she had no clue that the guy she continued to chat up was all but salivating over her. Was she too nervous about their time together to notice the attention? Good, that meant they were on equal footing. He was nervous, too. Nervous this week wouldn't be enough to convince Chloe that they were meant to be together, not apart.

As they reached their floor, Merrick let Chloe go before him. After she walked a few feet down the hall, he leaned toward the bellhop and gritted out, "Do you have worker's comp?"

"Uh, yeah, I guess so, why?"

"Stare at her chest one more time, you're going to need it."

The kid's eyes grew wide and he started to stammer.

Merrick cut him off. "How about you just stick to doing your job."

He nodded vehemently. "Y-yes, sir. No problem."

As they caught up to Chloe, she frowned and asked, "Was there a problem?"

Merrick smiled and patted her back. "Nope, I just had to set a few things straight. We're all good."

Chloe shrugged. As they reached the door to their suite, she let out a shuddering sigh and closed her eyes tight. "I still can't believe we're really here."

Merrick heard the desperation, the longing, in his wife's voice, and for the hundredth time that day he wanted to kick himself in the ass for letting things get to this point. He pulled her against his body and wrapped his arms around her, hugging her tight as he opened the door.

Their room was a corner suite. It wasn't the most private area of the resort, but on such short notice it was all that was available. The balcony gave them a beautiful view of the beach and ocean beyond. Chloe would like to have breakfast there, he thought. The bellhop opened a set of double doors to his left, and Merrick's libido roared to life. He knew what awaited them. A spacious bedroom with a king canopy bed complete with goose down duvets. He imagined Chloe surrounded by all that soft cotton, wrapped in his arms as the morning sun slowly brought them awake. The living room held all the luxuries of home. A desk and even high speed Internet access, which he wouldn't be using considering this wasn't going to be a working vacation. The refrigerator and personal bar might come in handy, though. He remembered their honeymoon night. He'd stocked the fridge with bottles of merlot and plates of cheese. Hell, they hadn't even bothered leaving the bed that night.

The bellhop left their luggage at the end of the bed and

practically ran from the room before Merrick could tip him. Smart kid.

"I can't believe we're here," Chloe said again.

Merrick held her tighter. "Believe it, baby. This is only the beginning. Everything is going to be different from here on out."

"I hope you're right, Merrick. I really do."

For the first time he noted a tinge of hope in her voice instead of emptiness. As far as he was concerned, it was a step in the right direction.

Chapter Five

"Because I want to, damn it, that's why."

Chloe rolled her eyes at Merrick's reason for wanting to shower with her. "It would be faster if you'd just let me finish."

"I'm not leaving, so deal with it."

"We're never going to get to dinner if you don't leave, Merrick."

"Fuck dinner. I want to wash you, so scoot over. Besides, let's not forget the deal. I'm in charge."

"Yes, you're in charge...of our fun. This is a shower."

"And a shower can be mighty fun."

Chloe wasn't sure why she continued to resist. As husband and wife they'd showered together hundreds of times. This time it seemed so different, as if it were the first time. A virgin on prom night would be less jumpy, for crying out loud!

"Fine, but if we don't make our reservations, don't blame me."

His grin was one of pure male arrogance. "Duly noted."

Chloe tried not to drool when Merrick yanked his shirt off and tossed it to the bathroom floor. As he undid the fly of his jeans and slid them and his black boxers down his powerful thighs, she gave up on maintaining control all together. God, he was gorgeous. His muscled behind faced her, and if she leaned toward him a few inches, she could take a bite out of his delicious flesh. He straightened and turned toward her. His cock was huge. As she watched, it seemed to get even bigger. As her gaze snared his, he grinned. She lit up like a Christmas tree.

"Those pretty eyes are devouring me right now, babe."

She pushed her wet hair behind her shoulder and tried not to let his sweet, hard body get to her...too much. "I can't help if I like what I see."

"I like what I see, too. A lot," he growled.

He stepped into the tub with her. Chloe moved to the side to give him room. He was twice her size and he took up most of the tub. Not that she was complaining. She couldn't remember the last time her husband had taken the time to shower with her. Too long. Much too long.

"You're so beautiful, Chloe. Inside and out."

His words and the sincerity behind them filled her heart with warmth. "You haven't told me that for a very long time. It's nice to hear compliments from you."

He slid the backs of his fingers down her wet arm, leaving little goose bumps in his wake. "You make me want to slay dragons and shower you with diamonds," he murmured. "I'm sorry I've been so wrapped up in work. I need to explain about that, but first I want to show you how much I've missed you. May I?"

He'd melted her completely. She'd become a useless puddle of pudding at his feet.

"Yes," she capitulated, "I think I'd like that very much."

He placed two fingers against her lips. "Shh, it's okay, baby. We're going to take our time, go real slow. I have a need to experience my wife to the fullest tonight."

She removed his fingers and asked, "What about dinner?" She didn't really care about food, but she should at least ask, for his sake.

"Screw dinner," he muttered.

As his mouth came crashing down on hers, Chloe fell against him, relishing the sensation of her nipples against the solid wall of his chest. At once he was everywhere, his arms sturdy and protective around her. He cupped her ass in his palms, lifted and pulled her tighter against his lethal strength. His hands squeezed, and she laughed. "Merrick, that tickles!"

"I know. Thought I'd forgotten, huh?"

Chloe feared he'd forgotten a lot of things about her, but she didn't want to reveal so much of her inner turmoil. "Well, you must admit it's not your typical ticklish spot."

"There's not a damn thing typical about your ass, Chloe. It's sexy as hell." He squeezed her flesh again, and she let loose a string of giggles. "When you giggle like that it turns me on like you wouldn't believe."

She liked the thought of Merrick turned on because of her. "What else turns you on?" she prompted.

"The cleft in your chin," he easily answered. His tongue came out and touched the little indentation. Her body flooded with liquid heat.

"Is that all?" she managed between pants.

"The length of your neck. You have a regal bearing, and your neck just begs to be kissed and nibbled."

He proceeded to prove his point by angling his head and teasing the side of her neck with his lips. He slid her wet hair out of the way and skimmed his tongue up and down her flesh, directly over her vein. He bit down and her pussy pulsed and swelled with need. Her hands clutched at his shoulders, fingernails biting into flesh and muscle. She closed her eyes and gave herself over to the moment. His mouth drifted lower, sliding over the tops of her breasts. When he kissed each nipple with tender affection, her legs shook with anticipation.

"The bellhop eyed your sweet tits like a mocha latte. Pissed me off," he gritted out. "But I have to admit, the kid has a good eye. You do look delicious, baby."

He cupped her left breast, brought it to his lips and sucked as much flesh as he could into his warm mouth. His tongue teased, his teeth grazed. She arched against him, mashing her other sensitive peak against his stubbled cheek. He cupped her right breast, flicked his thumb over the hard bud. Arrows of pleasure shot clear to her core. She hungered to make love to him. To feel him sinking deep inside her heat where she needed him so badly. The ache built and built until she whimpered and begged, shameless in her desire.

Merrick released her breast and pulled back. He stared up at her with such intensity her body vibrated as if stroked.

"Soon, baby, real soon, I promise. First, I need a taste. I've lived too long without your honey sliding over my tongue. I need to suck that tempting little pussy of mine."

She was beyond denying either of them. "Oh, God, yes."

Merrick's hungry grin had her nerve endings rioting out of control. He slid slowly to his knees, his gaze holding her immobile. The hot spray from the shower pelted them both. Merrick's body glistened, his muscles even more pronounced than before, his dark hair slicked back away from the harsh planes of his face.

Her husband. Her lover. Her everything.

Chloe became aware of the glaring truth in that moment. No matter what happened, her body would always be his to command, her heart his to hold.

He nudged her legs wider and clutched onto her thighs. Chloe sucked in a breath, knowing the pleasure only he could coax forth.

As his gaze snagged hers and held, she rested her palms on his shoulders and waited for that first delicious touch. He prolonged the moment and time seemed to stand still. Even in such a submissive position, Merrick still held power like none other. As he leaned forward and kissed her clit, they both groaned.

"No one will ever take you from me."

She wanted to protest, to let him know she had a mind of her own and would do what she had to do to keep her sanity, but his lips rubbing back and forth over her labia stopped her assertions. She couldn't think, couldn't grab onto a single skittering thought. She stopped trying to think and concentrated on feeling.

Merrick used his mouth with an expert's skill. His tongue dipped inside her heat, swirled around and came back out again.

"Fucking delicious," he murmured.

He sat back and removed his hands from her thighs, then used his thumbs to open her. His eyes on her there always made her hyper-aware of her femininity. Merrick always seemed to take such pleasure in looking at her intimate flesh before he took a taste, as if enthralled by the shape and texture of her body.

"Why do you do that?"

He licked his lips and smiled. "Do what?"

Chloe's cheeks filled with heat. She hadn't meant to ask. "You always look at me there," she explained. "It makes me nervous."

"Because you're beautiful," he admitted, his tone rough with arousal. "Every inch is beauty to me. God is surely an artist because you, my pretty wife, are a work of art."

Chloe's heart swelled. His words made perfect sense because she felt the same about him.

As his head descended on her, she clutched more tightly onto his wide shoulders. She knew what to expect and she craved it. His hot breath touched her first. She moaned aloud, and he blew a draft of air over her clitoris. She widened her stance, which gave him better access. She thought she might've pleaded a little, but she couldn't be certain. His tongue touched, ignited a fire inside that had burned white-hot for months.

He flicked over her swollen nether lips several times then sucked her clit into his mouth. She went wild, bucking against his face, aching so badly for his touch, his burning touch. He doubled his assault on her body and slid his middle finger deep inside her tight sheath. Her inner muscles squeezed him tight, as if loath to let him go. He growled. The deep timbre of his voice traveled over her clit and went straight to her womb. He lifted away, slid a second finger inside her pussy and pushed her to the very limit of control.

"Come for me. Let me feel you go up in flames, Chloe."

She couldn't speak, could barely keep her heart from leaping out of her chest. Merrick leaned in and licked once, twice, then pumped her fast and hard with his fingers. The last thread of her control snapped, and she flew over that invisible precipice that only Merrick could find.

He licked her flesh once more and cupped her mound in a gentle hold. "I've missed this pussy, baby. I've missed watching you go wild for my eyes alone."

"I never went anywhere. You were the one who left *me*."

He clenched his jaw and stood. His eyes held a wealth of

questions. When he only left the tub and held out a hand for her, surprise shot through her. Merrick never let a subject drop so easily.

"Come," he demanded, "the water's getting cold and what I have planned should be done in a bed anyway."

Chloe took his hand and let him help her out of the tub. She stood still while he dried her off, luxuriating in the attention. After he quickly towel-dried his own body, he bent at the knees and lifted her into his arms, startling a yelp out of her.

"It's not that big a suite, Merrick. I can walk just fine."

He stared down at her, his eyes glittering with arousal and just a hint of anger. "I want to hold my wife in my arms. Is that such a crime?"

Contrite, Chloe clasped her arms around his neck and held on. She'd been fighting him at every turn from the moment they'd landed. She'd agreed to this vacation. It wasn't fair to act as if she were here against her will.

She leaned down and placed a gentle kiss to his chest, enjoying the strength of his pecs. "Of course not," she murmured. As Chloe relaxed against him, she could've sworn Merrick shuddered.

They were both wound much too tight. It'd be a miracle if they didn't burn down the hotel with the heat of their passion!

Chapter Six

"I want to know something, Chloe," Merrick said, as he held his wife in his arms and walked into the bedroom.

"Yes?"

"And I want you to tell me the truth. Will you do that?"

"Of course."

He glanced down at her, noting the way she clutched her hands around his neck. She was still so shy with him, even after two years of marriage and everything they'd just done. A lifetime together and he'd probably never figure her out.

Merrick set her on her feet and watched her cross her arms over her chest. If she thought she was hiding anything, she was way off the mark.

He entwined his fingers with hers, enjoying the feel of her delicate flesh. She trembled, and Merrick wondered if it was from fear or excitement? He thought—hoped—it was the latter.

"It's been a long time for you, hasn't it, babe?"

Her cheeks grew pink. "Yes, but you already know that."

"And what did you do with yourself on those nights when you felt too warm, too excited to sleep, baby? Those nights when I was too busy working to tend to my aching wife."

"You mean did I...pleasure myself?" He nodded. "Yes. I am human, Merrick. I have needs the same as any other woman."

He cocked his head to the side. "I should have been there. Taking care of you."

"As I would have taken care of you."

The image of Chloe on her knees tonguing and sucking his cock filled his mind. He groaned.

He reached out and stroked her left nipple, then pinched it between his finger and thumb. She sucked in a breath and moaned at the small contact.

"Did you sink your pretty fingers inside that hot pussy? Did you use the vibrator I bought you?"

Chloe looked down, around, anywhere but directly at him.

"Tell me," he coaxed.

"I don't know what you want me to say."

He narrowed his eyes and spoke in a soft command. "I want to know how you pleasured yourself. In fact, I want you to show me."

She quirked an eyebrow. "You mean you want me to masturbate for you?"

His lips curved upward at her stunned expression. "Yeah. I want you to get up on the bed and show me." He released her hand and cupped her pussy, his other fingers still plying her nipple. "Let me see you tease this delectable body into a frenzy. This is your chance to show me just exactly what I've been missing."

Chloe opened her mouth, but no sound came out. Time to show her one of the items he'd brought along for their pleasure.

Merrick released his hold on her body. She licked her lips and clenched her fists at her sides as he stepped away. He went to his suitcase and unzipped the outside compartment, then brought out a small bullet vibrator. He turned around and showed it to her.

"You brought it with you?"

He shrugged. "You left it behind when you moved out. I thought it might come in handy."

She blinked as if trying to assimilate all that was happening, then took the vibrator out of his hand and stared at it. Merrick moved behind her and nudged her forward. When she didn't budge an inch, he chuckled.

He leaned down and whispered, "Drive me crazy, baby. Make me pay for all those nights when I spent time at the office instead of on top of you, fucking you, making you come all over my dick."

He wrapped an arm around her, placed his palm on her left breast, directly over her heart. It beat erratically. Merrick could feel her breaths coming too fast. He'd gotten to her. He nudged her forward again, and this time she complied.

As Chloe stepped forward and crawled onto the bed, Merrick's adrenaline shot up. He pictured her spread out, hand between her thighs, playing with her own soft, creamy flesh. It drove him a little crazy. Suddenly, he wanted to skip the show and get right to the main event. It'd be hard, fast. He'd bury his cock so deep inside her she wouldn't be able to walk away. Ever.

But he didn't. It was imperative he take it slow with Chloe. To experience every single ounce of pleasure. Maybe then she wouldn't leave him.

As she positioned herself in the center of the bed and spread her legs a few inches, Merrick realized she had her eyes closed. He didn't want her distancing herself. He needed her to know exactly whom she was with and where they were.

"Chloe, look at me."

Her eyelids fluttered open and she turned her head toward him. Her sensual gaze trapped him. She was so aroused she nearly left him scorched. If he had any doubts about what they were going to do, the hot look Chloe gave him squelched them.

"You're excited aren't you, baby?" Merrick stepped forward, his cock at eye level.

She glanced down his body and licked her lips. "Yes," she breathed out.

Her husky one word reply let him know it wouldn't take her long before she came for him again. "Why?" Merrick asked, as he slid a single finger over her arm.

"Because I've imagined this very scenario."

Now that hadn't been what he'd expected to hear. "You have?"

"Yes. There have been so many nights I imagined you walking in on me. I fantasized about you making love to me afterwards. Cherishing me. Staying with me."

Jesus. He'd been so blind. "I do cherish you, Chloe."

She nodded. "I know you love me. I never questioned that."

What she didn't say was that she'd gotten tired of waiting for him to treat her like a wife instead of a piece of furniture. His thoughts stuttered to a halt as she grasped his wrist and brought his hand to her right breast.

"Touch me while you watch, Merrick."

Her nipple hardened beneath his palm. "You're so fucking sexy, sweetheart. I can't get enough."

He massaged his hand in slow circles over her creamy tit, squeezed the tip between his index finger and thumb, relishing the way she arched toward him. Her fingertips came up to touch his chest, but Merrick grabbed onto her wrist and held her away from him. "Show me," he demanded.

She smiled up at him as she slowly, calculatedly, spread her legs wider. He could see the cream of her sex, the swollen labia and tempting little clit peeking out. Open and glistening. Chloe's luscious pussy had his cock so full and ready it hurt to stand there and not jump onto the bed. He longed to forget everything he'd just said, beg for a taste of her juices. Just one lick. One suck. Hell, he'd give his left nut to drown in her sweet scent, feel her wet heat in his mouth. Watch her come as he sucked her dry.

She slid the toy between her legs, careful to keep her gaze on him. He fisted his hands at his sides in an effort for control. He heard a low buzzing sound as she clicked on the tiny massager. A smile curved her lips. Christ, what had he started?

Merrick's muscles flexed with the urge to take her, rough, the need to make love to his wife nearly too strong to ignore. His dick was as hard as a fucking tire iron and he needed to slide it between Chloe's succulent pussy lips. He vowed not to take her like a rutting buck. Correction: his brain didn't want that sort of coarse lovemaking; his cock, on the other hand, wanted to be inside Chloe's tight cunt. It didn't much matter how that came about.

As she touched the bulbous tip of her massager to her clit, Merrick licked his lips and knew a momentary pang of jealousy. Damn it, he was jealous over a piece of vibrating plastic!

He stepped closer, bumping his shins into the box springs. His legs weighed a ton, as if he'd just run five miles. As he moved closer, Chloe rewarded him with a siren's smile. She knew exactly the effect she had on him. She enjoyed the hell out of it, too. He drank in the sight of her as her breathing increased, her composure slipping a little more. The massager glided over her clit, back and forth, then dipped between her pussy lips. Her lower body started a sweet, gyrating rhythm that had his cock dripping with precome. As she cupped her free hand over one round breast, plucked and tugged at her own nipple, Merrick let loose a low groan. Enough was enough.

No man could stand such torture.

He leaned down and touched the inside of her thigh. He smoothed his hand toward the sopping wet center he craved so badly. Merrick's pounding heartbeat nearly drowned out everything else.

"I want to watch you, Merrick," Chloe pleaded in a throaty purr that caressed his flesh. "I want your hand on your cock, pumping and squeezing. Do it now, before I come. Please."

Merrick needed no more provocation. With his legs braced apart, he wrapped a tight fist around his heavy length and pumped, slowly, up and down. Chloe's eyes grew dark with passion. Her lips parted and her small pink tongue darted out, licking, as if imagining his taste. He watched the movement, sensing that teasing stroke on his cock.

"Is this what you wanted, baby?" he asked. She nodded eagerly. He placed one palm on the bed and leaned down, then pressed his lips to hers. She opened eagerly. Merrick sank his tongue inside, licking and tasting her sweet flavor.

"Lift up a little and lick my cock, baby."

She never hesitated. Chloe kept a firm hold on her toy while she pushed herself toward him and licked his dripping tip. Merrick lost it. Her touch. Her sighs. It was all too damn much.

"Fuck, I have to taste you. I'm sorry, baby, I can't wait any longer."

He dropped to the floor at the side of the bed and pushed her massager out of the way, then pressed his mouth against her hot mound. Merrick took her clit between his teeth and flicked it back and forth. He had the crazy notion that he'd found home. This was where he belonged, not some stuffy office building.

He suckled and nibbled. Chloe's fingers sank into his hair.

She grasped his scalp and held him against her intimate flesh as she took her own pleasure. He licked at her, absorbing the sounds of Chloe's hoarse cries and whimpers. She bucked against his face and came suddenly, wildly, screaming his name over and over again. The sweetest music he'd ever heard.

He kissed her swollen nub and stood, then placed one knee on the bed and straddled her.

"I want your lips wrapped around my cock."

Chloe's eyes opened, a dreamy expression on her face, and held out her arms. "Come up here."

"Fuck, yeah."

Even as a gangly teenager, Merrick hadn't been this turned on. Somehow, Chloe had turned the tables. She seemed to be orchestrating their little symphony now. He stared at her lying on the bed, her body splayed wide, not a care in the world, and the sight touched his heart. She made such a tempting picture with the secret smile curving her pretty lips and the rosy afterglow of her climax. In that moment, Merrick knew that whatever Chloe wanted, Chloe was liable to get.

Merrick placed his hands on the headboard behind her and crawled up her body, straddling her face. His eyes glazed over as she stared at his cock bobbing an inch from her mouth. She licked her lips and closed the gap between them, before kissing the swollen purple tip.

"Oh, hell, Chloe, you'll be the death of me."

She hummed and wrapped her arms around his thighs, then probed the slit in his tip with her tongue. Merrick bucked and clutched onto the headboard until his knuckles turned white. He knew what would happen next. His sweet Chloe would take him straight to heaven.

Chapter Seven

Nothing tasted quite as delicious as Merrick. That special blend of spice and masculine heat revved Chloe's engines every time. She gave into temptation and licked the underside of his shaft. He groaned and pressed his cock closer. She knew his intent. He wanted her to take him into her mouth, suck him to the back of her throat, and let him come all over her voracious tongue. She wanted that too, but Chloe needed to make the man squirm a little first.

She released her hold on his thighs and wrapped both her hands around the base of his cock, then pumped up and down. She laved him with her tongue, over and over. Her body began the slow climb again, aching and ready. In her mind, she saw him filling her, stretching her tight channel and pounding into her so hard they both saw stars.

"Yeah, baby, just like that. Make love to my cock."

Chloe used one hand to cup his heavy sac. Merrick jerked as if burned. She smiled before lifting his cock out of the way and bringing his balls to her mouth. She sucked one in and let her teeth graze over the smooth skin. Merrick shouted her name, his pleasure becoming her own. She popped it out of her mouth, then showered the same attention on the other soft orb.

"Bite down," he demanded, "just a little. Let me feel that squeeze, sweetheart."

Chloe let her lips close around his sac. Merrick's fingers dug into her scalp, holding her against him. She pulled back and peered up at him. His lids were barely open, and the feral expression on his face had her trembling. For months she'd felt abandoned and ignored. In this single moment in time, Chloe had Merrick's full attention and she basked in it. Keeping it would be the tricky part.

Chloe wrapped her fingers around the base of his hard, pulsing length and brought it to her lips. She rubbed his tip back and forth, letting the moisture coat her mouth.

"Open, baby. Let me fuck that hot little mouth."

Beyond denying him, Chloe parted her lips. Merrick took over at once. He pushed his hips forward an inch and filled her mouth with the swollen head of his cock. The width of him had her stretching her lips wider to accommodate for his size. She closed her eyes and drew him in an inch at a time, until at last he touched the back of her throat. Chloe wrapped her arms around his hips and dug her fingers into his buttocks. Merrick went wild. He flexed his hips and pushed forward, then back, fucking her mouth. When she released her hold on his left ass cheek and cupped his balls, he suddenly pulled out. Chloe frowned up at him.

"Open your mouth. I want to watch my come spurt all over your tongue, and you're to keep it there until I say."

Chloe didn't need him to order her. She loved his particular flavor. She opened her mouth, and Merrick was there, pumping his cock with his fist. His fingers dug deep into her hair, pulling almost painfully as he exploded, pouring hot creamy fluid all over her tongue and teeth.

Merrick pulled back, his gaze trained on the pool of creamy fluid inside her mouth. "Mmm, that's sexy, baby." He paused, then added, "Now you can swallow."

She closed her mouth and swallowed her husband's salty fluid. Sweat glistened on Merrick's pecs and abs, and his eyes had darkened with arousal as he hovered over her. Her heart did a little flip at the sight of her gorgeous husband. The primal image would always stay with her.

"You have the most wicked way of turning me inside out, baby."

Chloe liked the sound of that. It told her she gave him something no other could. "I think that's a mutual feeling."

He lay down on his side next to her, his semi-hard cock pressing into her thigh. "But I'm not through with you. I want more. I'll always want more from you, Chloe."

She knew that couldn't be true. The past several months proved he might want it to be true, but the reality was far different.

"Three months," she bit out.

He'd propped his head on his hand and started to stroke a finger over her breasts and ribcage when her statement seemed to register. He froze.

"What?"

"Three months since you last made love to me."

His cheeks reddened. "No way has it been three months. That's not possible."

She flung her arm over her eyes and muttered, "It is. Believe me, I counted."

Merrick's fingers wrapped around her wrist and tugged, forcing her to look at him. "You could have approached me. Desire between a husband and wife is a two-way street, Chloe."

That was the wrong thing to say. She sat up and pointed a finger at his chest. "You think I didn't try? Oh, I tried all right! Over and over. I even worried that you had someone else!"

Merrick cupped her jaw and frowned. "You can't be serious. Baby, there's only you. I swear on my life I've never even come close to cheating."

"I know," she admitted. "In my heart I knew you'd never cheat on me. Still, that left me with no explanation as to why you wouldn't touch me. Why we hadn't made love." Her voice broke and tears filled her eyes. "Why, Merrick?"

He swiped a tear away with his thumb. "I'm not making excuses, but I didn't intentionally push you away. I've been consumed with the business. Making it something that would withstand the test of time is very important to me. I'm sorry that need overshadowed the most vital thing in my life: you."

"I'm proud of your hard work, but that doesn't explain this rift."

Merrick pulled her close and placed the gentlest of kisses to her lips. He lifted away a mere inch and murmured, "I have a lot of things to explain to you." He kissed her cheek. "A helluva lot to make up for." He lay back on the bed and brought her on top of him as he went. "But right now I need to show you how much I've missed you. Give me tonight. Tomorrow I'll tell you everything."

He placed a chaste kiss to her lips, and Chloe surrendered. "Tomorrow. Promise me."

"Tomorrow, baby, I promise."

"Then quit messing around and kiss me like you mean it."

He chuckled. "Yes, ma'am."

Merrick cupped the back of her head and pulled her down for a bone-melting mating of lips. He crushed his mouth to hers and teased her lips apart, their tongues dueling. Chloe drifted on a sea of desire as Merrick took his time sucking on her tongue. His calloused palms skated up her back and held her close. She pushed her breasts against his chest and rubbed her hardened peaks back and forth. Merrick groaned into her mouth and ground his hips into the juncture between her thighs. She pulled away and sat atop him. Gazes locked, she positioned his cock and let him barely breach her entrance, torturing them both.

"Goddamn you're tight. I'm burning up here, babe."

Chloe's thighs trembled. "I love the way you feel inside me. You're so hard and strong."

"And you're so fucking soft I want to sink into your sweet little cunt and never leave," he growled. "Ride me, Chloe."

"Yes," she breathed out. Chloe levered herself with her hands on his chest and slowly sank onto his heavy, swollen erection. He stretched her inner walls, stroked sensitive tissues.

He pulled her down and cupped her breast. "Mmm, come to Daddy," he urged in a husky whisper that moved along her nerve endings like the stroke of a feather. "So good, so fucking perfect."

Chloe couldn't speak around the lump in her throat. Her husband's gaze held her captive. She was so wet and slick, yet her body still milked his engorged length. When she whimpered, he smoothed his palm up her spine in a soothing caress. "Easy. We have all the time in the world."

"I never want it to end, Merrick, never."

"And it won't," he vowed.

She threw her head back and began moving up and down, before grinding her hips into his and allowing his cock to sink even deeper.

"Yeah, do that again."

She repeated the movement, rising up until just the bulbous head was nestled between her pussy lips, then slid down again, fusing their bodies together. Merrick groaned his approval, his gaze never leaving her face. His hands slid over her body, touching everywhere, as if reacquainting himself with her every curve and valley. Chloe luxuriated in having his total concentration.

She squeezed her inner muscles and Merrick's hips shot upward. The sweet lover disappeared and in his place lay a wild and uninhibited warrior. Her husband's primitive nature took over. He began thrusting and retreating, hard and fast, driving them both to the ragged edge of desire.

"Merrick!" she cried out.

He lifted up, wrapped his arms around her and buried his face against her neck. "I've got you, baby."

His lips caressed as he drove his cock deep. Chloe met him thrust for thrust. Merrick found the special spot on her neck that always drove her crazy and sucked her overheated skin. She dug her fingers into his hair and held him close. His arms tightened around her as he pushed in and out, fucking her tight channel.

The fire inside her core burned hotter and hotter until her pussy clutched his cock like a fiery fist. He pulled back and thrust forward one more time. Chloe lost it. Merrick kept his arms locked around her shoulders as she burst all around him, screaming his name. The orgasm went on and on, Merrick seemed intent to pull every last drop of pleasure from her.

After she came down from the euphoric high, Merrick lifted his head. "Look at me, beautiful."

Chloe opened her eyes and stared at her husband. "Come for me, Merrick," she murmured.

"Anything you say, sweetheart." He thrust his hips upward once, twice, three times before he filled her with his hot seed. The swiftness of it shocked her to the core. He'd been waiting, riding that shaky edge until she found her own completion.

Chloe couldn't drag her gaze away as Merrick's entire demeanor changed, became more intense.

"Do you see how we fit? Do you feel me inside you?"

"Yes, Merrick."

"No other will ever fill you like me. This isn't about chemistry or body size either. It goes deeper than that. This is about love."

"And no other will ever fit you like me?" she asked, hesitant about this new side to her husband.

"Exactly. I will not let you go." His arms crushed her to him, his head buried in the valley between her breasts.

She pushed his sweat-soaked hair away from his face. "We don't always get what we want, Merrick. It's called free will."

He nuzzled her bosom, kissed each of her nipples before leaning back. "Yes, free will. But I happen to know a secret, baby."

"And what's that?"

"I know you, inside and out. If you really thought I was beyond help, you wouldn't have hesitated to dump my workaholic ass."

Damn. He had her there. She *had* thought he was worth the effort and she did think their marriage worth saving. Merrick hadn't neglected her on purpose. She knew that in her heart. The question remained as to why he'd put her on the backburner.

He'd claimed to tell her everything tomorrow. They'd talk then. She'd finally get some long overdue answers.

Chapter Eight

Merrick sat at the little table on the terrace of their suite, soaking in the fresh morning breeze as he read the latest headlines. He took a sip of the fresh coffee that had arrived moments earlier. He'd always been an early riser, but he'd actually slept until eight. He couldn't believe the time when he'd looked at the clock. He hadn't slept past six in the morning since his college days.

It hadn't been easy to leave the warmth of Chloe's naked body. She'd been draped over him like a human blanket, but he'd had a lot of thinking to do. Things to plan. Today he'd promised an explanation for his obsessively focused attitude toward work. Christ, he'd practically abandoned her. His pride stung when he thought of how he'd treated her. The most precious thing in his life, and yet his need to prove himself had overshadowed that fact. There could be no changing the past, though. All he could do now was prove he'd never neglect her again. He only hoped she gave him a second chance.

A rustle of fabric behind him caught his attention and pulled him out of his thoughts. He turned in his chair to see Chloe standing in the doorway. Her long hair lay in tangled waves over her shoulders, down past her breasts. Her cream-colored silk robe delineated her sleek lines and full, rounded hips. She could wear a burlap sack and it still wouldn't hide curves like hers.

His mouth watered.

Merrick held out his hand and murmured, "Come here, angel."

Chloe padded barefoot across the patio, rubbing her sleepy eyes. "How come you didn't wake me?"

He chuckled and pulled her onto his lap. "And risk a limb?"

She smacked his chest. "I'm not that bad and you know it."

Chloe grumbled and groused until she had at least two cups of coffee. "You don't do mornings well. Remember the time right after we were married? I decided to wake you and surprise you with breakfast in bed. Big mistake."

She laughed. "I didn't shove the tray in your face on purpose. It was an involuntary reaction."

He smoothed his palm down her back and slid his fingers over the top of her ass. "It wasn't my face that got drenched. I ended up with scrambled eggs and grape juice all over my boxers. And that juice was cold as hell, too."

Her eyes darkened with arousal. "But I cleaned you up afterwards."

He angled his head and kissed her lightly. "Mmm, yes you did. I enjoyed your apology very much."

Chloe started to leave his lap, but Merrick clamped his arm around her tighter. "Going somewhere?"

"I need to shower. I feel all...sticky."

He let his palm drift up her thigh, pushing her robe apart as he went. The instant he felt her soft curls, his semi-erect cock stood to full attention. He slid a finger between her pussy lips and encountered creamy heat. "You're aroused."

Chloe sighed and leaned back. "Sitting on your lap does that to me."

"I'm very glad."

Merrick wiggled his index finger deeper. The clutch of her inner muscles had him pushing his dick into her bottom. He needed to bury himself inside his wife's welcoming sheath. He pulled his finger free, then grasped onto her waist, turning her around until she straddled him. They didn't speak as he untied her robe and exposed her nude body in the soft morning light.

She made a grab for the robe. "What if someone sees us, Merrick?"

"Haven't you ever wanted to try something just a little bit naughty, Chloe?"

"I-I suppose."

He pushed her robe off her shoulders and watched it pool around her waist. Merrick looked over Chloe's shoulder and realized another couple in a hotel room adjacent to them watched their every move. Merrick's possessive instinct was to cover his wife from the other man's view, but he stopped himself. This was a week they'd always remember. Why not go a little wild? Besides, the other couple couldn't really see anything except Chloe's back. What they were doing would be obvious, but it'd be their imagination that filled in the blanks.

Merrick stroked the backs of his fingers over Chloe's left nipple and watched in fascination as it hardened before his eyes. He leaned forward and whispered into her ear, "We're being watched."

Chloe jerked as if he'd dashed her in the face with a glass of ice water. When she made a grab for the robe, he placed his hands over hers and stopped her. "Shh, relax. They can't see anything, not really. Let them watch."

Merrick detected Chloe's hesitant surrender in her guarded expression. "Are you sure they can't see anything?"

He glanced over her shoulder again. "Nothing but your

back. With the robe around your waist, they can't see anything *juicy*. And because we're sitting down, the railing provides some cover, too. They'll have to guess at what's going on."

Chloe's brow arched upward. "It won't be too hard to guess, Merrick." She paused and her gaze caught on something behind him. "I can see them in the glass."

He'd begun playing with a lock of her hair, enjoying the soft texture between his fingers, when her words registered. "The patio door?"

"Yes. I can just barely make out what they're wearing, but no real details."

"Let yourself go, baby. Trust me to take care of you."

Instead of answering, she wrapped her hands around his face and leaned forward. The barely-there caress of her lips did things to him, crazy things. That she initiated the kiss made him feel somehow triumphant. Merrick pulled her against his body, crushing his mouth to hers even as her supple breasts pressed against his chest. He slid his hands down her back and cupped her ass, fondling gently, careful not to push the robe away and risk exposing her lower half. He pushed his erection against her, but pulled back when he encountered cotton.

"Too many clothes," he muttered as he skimmed his fingers beneath the waistband of his boxers and released his cock. Skin touched skin. His blood raced. Her small palm coasted over his torso, down his abs, and grasped his heavy length.

Chloe took her time, smoothing her thumb back and forth over his dripping tip. As she lifted and positioned him right at the entrance to paradise, Merrick's chest tightened. She sat slowly, her body sucking him in inch by delicious inch until she'd embedded his dick deep.

"Christ, woman," Merrick groaned.

Chloe buried her head in the crook of his neck and rode

69

him with slow, sweet precision. Merrick glanced over to the other couple, ensuring they still had a modicum of privacy. He was shocked to the core when he saw the woman bent over the railing, her shirt gone, her lover pounding into her from behind. Her eyes were closed and her large breasts jiggled with each thrust. She said something incoherent, then her lover leaned down and kissed the side of her neck.

Merrick had a sudden need for privacy. What had seemed like a fun idea at first now felt intrusive. When Chloe squeezed her inner muscles, his worries were lost in the torrent of desire coursing through his body. His only thought was Chloe. What would his wife think of the erotic show playing out?

"Open your eyes and watch the glass," he demanded.

Chloe's lids shot up. He knew the instant she'd spotted the couple. Her cheeks filled with color, and she bit her lip, but she didn't look away. Merrick wrapped his arms around her waist and pulled her against him, further hiding her from curious eyes. He nibbled his way up her neck, playing with the sensitive spot behind her ear. Chloe moaned and moved faster. His gaze shot once more to the couple on the other terrace. This time the woman couldn't be seen. Her lover stood there, out in the open, pumping his own cock as he stared at the floor. Merrick realized the woman must be on her knees. He looked at Chloe. Her lips were parted, her chest heaving with exertion as she rode him. With her dreamy eyes closed, it was clear she was lost in her own sensations.

The sexy picture of his wife slowly fucking him into oblivion took Merrick over the top. He forgot about where they were and who might see. He braced his feet on the cement patio and pushed upward several times, fucking her tight cunt with hard, forceful thrusts. Chloe moaned and gripped his shoulders.

"Come, baby," he commanded

Chloe's body tightened, swelled. She arched her neck, and Merrick cupped the back of her head and slanted his mouth over hers, drinking in her wild cries. She wrapped her powerful legs tightly around the chair, squeezing him, sending him over a blissful cliff and straight into a blazing inferno. He drove into her pussy hard one last time and exploded, filling her with jets of hot come. Her body pulsed all around his cock, sucking him in farther, milking him dry. Chloe slumped against him, sated and exhausted.

"Are you determined to make up for three months of abstaining in a single twenty-four hour period?" she complained, breathless and still pulsing all around his still-hard length.

Merrick laughed at her disgruntled tone and glanced over at the other terrace. The couple had disappeared. He imagined awkwardly meeting them in the lobby or riding the same elevator later and laughed.

"What's so funny?"

"That other couple."

"Yeah?"

"It'd be downright weird riding in the elevator with them, wouldn't it?"

Chloe groaned and hid her face in his chest. "I'm taking the stairs," she mumbled.

He pulled her back and forced her to look at him. "It's twenty-three floors, babe."

Merrick tucked himself back into his boxers before helping her with her robe. She stood and glared down at him. "I'm in really good shape. It shouldn't be a problem."

He grabbed her hand as she started to walk away. "It was fun in a naughty sort of way. Admit it."

The ornery grin spreading over her face was reminiscent of the old Chloe. "Yeah, it was pretty fun," she admitted.

She walked back into the suite a little shakier than she'd walked out. His heart swelled. She'd started to relax a little. This would only be the beginning. By the end of the week, they'd be back on track. They had to be. The only other alternative scared the shit out of him.

Chapter Nine

"This is heavenly, Merrick. Thank you for taking me here."

Merrick smiled and swiped a strawberry from the bowl, then brought it to Chloe's lips. "Open up, sweetheart."

Chloe opened and let him slip the fresh berry into her mouth. She bit down and juice dribbled down her chin. Merrick leaned over her and licked at the sweet juice. "Delicious," he murmured. Chloe's heart raced at the gruff sound of her husband's voice. When Merrick was aroused, she was aroused. It was that simple.

She concentrated on not choking on the luscious fruit and looked out at the ocean. The Kapiolani Beach Park had everything a couple of tourists could want. Beautiful scenery, walking trails, beaches, and lots of spots to set up a picnic and bask in the sun. The weather was a perfect seventy-five degrees and sunny. Better yet, she had Merrick's undivided attention. It was time they finally talked.

Chloe sat up and placed the bowl of berries to the side. "You said last night you'd tell me everything. I'm ready to listen."

Merrick's hard, powerful body was spread out like a banquet next to her. The blissful expression on his face mesmerized her. As her words sank in, his face closed down. She couldn't tell what went through his mind.

He sat up, pulled one knee to his chest and pinned her with a hard stare. "Before I say anything, I want you to understand something. I love you. I love you more than anything in this world, Chloe. I hope someday you'll believe that."

Chloe couldn't speak around the lump in her throat. She only nodded and let him continue.

"When you and I met it was like instant combustion," he explained. "I melted anytime you came into a room. Your soft voice, your intelligent eyes. You ran the office with such confidence it was mesmerizing. I craved you from day one. It took some time, I admit, but I managed to forget about the rules I'd placed on myself about not getting involved with an employee. You were different. I knew it from the start. It was only a matter of time before we'd marry."

Chloe agreed wholeheartedly. She'd fallen in love the minute she'd met with the devastatingly handsome owner of Vaughn's Business Solutions. It *had* been only a matter of time before they were living in marital bliss. "Some people wait a lifetime for a love like ours."

"I know."

His smile didn't quite reach his eyes and that worried Chloe. "I'm listening," she prodded.

"Let me tell you about my family. Maybe you'll understand."

She frowned. "Your family? I love your family. Your mom is like a second mother to me."

"They're pretty great, huh?"

"Yes. I'm so thrilled that Blade and Lacey both found someone to love. Candice, Lacey and I are as close as sisters."

"Lacey and Blade are both damn determined people. They see something they want and they go after it. Blade's business is thriving. He hires on more employees every day. His reputation in construction is unsurpassed."

Chloe heard the note of pride in her husband's voice, but she was still confused. "What does any of this have to do with you and me?"

"It'll be clear, just let me finish, okay?"

She nodded.

"Lacey's doing pretty great herself. She has so many clients now she'll have to open her own gym soon."

Chloe had seen the proof first hand. Lacey's schedule was bursting with clients. She was almost constantly at the gym. "Lacey and Blade are both very driven. It seems to be a family trait."

Merrick stared out at the ocean. His entire body seemed ready for battle. "Blade leaves big shoes to fill," he muttered. "I love him. He's the best brother anyone could ask for, but it's not easy living in his shadow. Dad looks at him with pride and respect. He looks at me with..."

Chloe caught the misery in his voice, and her heart hurt for him. "He respects you. I know he does."

"Lacey and Blade both know their place in life," he continued. "I've always been the one who had to struggle for everything. In school, I studied twice as hard as Blade just to get a B. In college, Blade got into some boxing, he was great at it. His grades were top notch too. I, on the other hand, stayed up every night, drank more coffee than is healthy and passed with average grades. Hell, I think Mom and Dad were just glad I graduated."

Chloe had never known Merrick to feel inferior, and especially to Blade. She didn't have siblings so it was difficult to imagine. Her mother had always made her feel strong and intelligent, as if she were capable of anything. Her father, although emotionally distant, had told her more than once that she could do anything she set her mind to. He'd smile with pride and say she was just like her mother.

"But look at you now," she hastened to reassure him. "You own your own business and you're definitely more successful than Blade."

Merrick shrugged. "I'm not trying to make it a competition. I'm happy for Blade and his success. Anyway, that's not what I want to explain." He turned and pinned her with his gaze. Chloe's breath caught at the raw anguish on her husband's face. "I thought it would make me a better man when I hit my first million. That I'd finally earn some respect and I'd have my place in the family. I was so goddamn wrong. I've been kicking myself for not seeing it sooner."

"Seeing what?"

"You. I should've known how successful I'd become the instant you drifted into my life. I should've realized that losing you is the only thing that could make me a failure. Nothing else matters. Not money, not social status. Not my parents' approval."

Hearing her husband's confession and seeing the sincerity in his intelligent blue eyes turned her inside out. Tears spilled free, and her body shook with all the worry and fear and sadness she'd felt over the last six months. She swiped them away quickly, sensing Merrick had more to say.

"The first time you spoke of having babies scared the shit out of me."

Chloe had been prepared for nearly everything, but never that. She'd thought Merrick wanted children, too. The notion that he might not had never crossed her mind. "Don't you think I'd be a good mother?"

Merrick wrapped his fingers around her knee and stroked.

"Aw, angel, you'll make a wonderful mother. The best ever. I want children with you." His palm cupped her belly. "I want to watch your belly swell with my son or daughter. Hell, both," he growled. "You'll be sexy as hell pregnant."

Thank God, Chloe thought. Her stomach settled a little. "Then why the fear?"

"Because I started imagining being a father," he ground out.

Merrick stood and paced, hands in his pockets. Chloe took a moment to digest all Merrick had revealed. She thought back to that first time she'd mentioned wanting to get pregnant. She'd ached to fill their house with the laughter of a baby. With total clarity she could see that day in her head as if it were yesterday. Six months. She'd brought up the subject six months ago, right after breakfast on a Saturday morning. Immediately afterward, Merrick's schedule had filled with work. He'd literally poured every ounce of himself into the business. Deep down, she knew her husband would be the best father in the world, but how could she convince him when he seemed so insecure?

Chloe stood and went to him. She wrapped her arms around his middle and buried her nose in his navy blue t-shirt. He stood as still as a marble statue, as if afraid of letting himself be comforted. His arms slowly came around her shoulders, and soon his embrace was so tight she had to struggle to breathe.

When an elderly couple walked by and grinned, it immediately reminded Chloe of their very public surroundings. Chloe wiggled, and Merrick loosened his hold. He gazed down at her, his eyes so filled with worry it nearly broke her heart.

She cupped his cheek and smiled. "I know you'll be a terrific father." He started to protest, but she placed two fingers against his lips and said, "But only when you're ready. I never meant to pressure you. Having a baby is a decision we both need to make."

Merrick didn't speak. He simply leaned down and fastened his lips to hers as if desperate for her taste. Her muscles went into instant meltdown as she gave him every ounce of love she could give. As his tongue found its way inside her mouth, Chloe groaned, enjoying his stimulating flavor. When Merrick broke the kiss and stared down at her, Chloe had to force her raging hormones back into their cage.

"I don't deserve you, Chloe," he said, caressing her cheek. "I never did."

Merrick's eyes were over-bright, as if close to tears. Chloe had never seen her husband so overwhelmed with emotion. Knowing he was close to losing control slashed at her soul.

"That's nonsense. All these worries you have are unfounded, Merrick. You're a good man and everyone knows it...except you."

"If I'm so good, why is it I nearly lost you?"

Chloe stepped out of Merrick's arms and started to gather up their trash and leftovers. "The hotel did a wonderful job putting together the picnic, don't you think?"

Merrick bent to help. "Yeah, but why are you avoiding my question?"

Chloe stopped and stared at the used napkin in her hand. "Because I'm not sure our marriage is out of the woods." Her gaze locked with his as she gave him the bold truth. "I understand better now and I appreciate your honesty. I wish I'd known six months ago how you really felt. It might have made a difference." She tossed the napkin into a paper bag. "I'm so afraid that when this week is over you'll go right back to working around the clock, and where does that leave me?

Where does that leave us?"

Merrick clasped Chloe's face in his palms. "That won't happen. On my honor, that won't happen. I know it's hard to believe now, considering my track record, but you have to have faith."

"I want so badly to believe you and that scares me."

Merrick rubbed his thumb over her bottom lip and murmured, "Every couple has problems, babe. There is no such thing as a perfect marriage."

"I know, I do, and I never asked for perfection, just a flesh and blood husband."

He angled his head and kissed her. Chloe's knees went weak. He could so easily turn her inside out. It seemed so unfair at times. As if he had more command over her body than she.

Chloe pulled back an inch and watched him lick his lips. Even that small action drove her imagination wild.

"We have something going for us that a lot of couples don't," he stated. "We're in love. And I happen to think it's the forever kind of thing. You're not ready to walk away from what we have together."

She couldn't deny his words. The fact she'd come to Hawaii with him was proof enough that she was willing to work it out. What neither of them said aloud was that she had taken the first step. The hardest step. She'd left him. At one time she would have sworn she'd never make such a bold move.

Chloe finished gathering the trash in silence and together they folded the blanket. Merrick slung it over his shoulder as Chloe searched out a waste bin for their trash.

Hand in hand they headed back to the hotel, her mind a jumble of thoughts and feelings. Merrick was the first to break the silence.

"Let's go parasailing."

Definitely *not* what she expected. "Parasailing?"

"Why not? We can drop off the blanket and get our swimsuits on and be out on the water within the hour."

Chloe laughed, feeling a lot more carefree than she had in a long time. "Let's do it!"

The sexy glint of arousal in Merrick's eyes kick-started her heart. "I love it when you get that wild look, babe."

Chloe pulled Merrick to a stop, rose up on her tiptoes and covered his lips with her own. Merrick stepped forward, aligning their bodies. He tilted his head to take over the kiss. His tongue probed the seam and she parted, aching for his flavor on her tongue. The kiss seemed to last forever. Someone yelled out, "*Get a room,*" effectively yanking them out of their erotic haze. Merrick dropped his hands and stepped back. Chloe couldn't catch her breath.

"If we weren't out in the open..." Merrick groaned.

Oh, wow. She could only imagine.

Chapter Ten

It'd been a week filled with revelations. After the day in the park, Merrick seemed determined to wring every ounce of fun he could out of their trip. They'd gone parasailing, which she'd discovered she loved. The heights had made her a bit shaky at first, but with Merrick right beside her she'd gotten over those initial jitters. They'd gone out on a jet ski the next day and she'd gotten a bit too pink from the sun. Chloe hadn't cared, though; she'd been having way too much fun. Who knew she had a thing for speed? She'd already begun working out a plan to buy herself one. Unrealistic and way out of character, but who cared? Sometimes a girl needed to have a little fun.

Three days into their vacation, Merrick had arranged for her to have time at the hotel spa. The full treatment—massage, manicure, pedicure and facial. It'd been heavenly. Afterwards, he'd made love to her for hours. In the last five days, they'd made love in the shower, the bed, the patio and there'd even been a wild moment against the door to their suite.

This was to be their final evening. Chloe's legs shook with nerves. When she'd agreed to the trip, she'd been ready for a mental breakdown. Her heart had been in tatters as she watched her marriage fall apart. Six days of bliss with Merrick had changed them both. She still didn't know where they were supposed to go from here, but she had two things she didn't have before: hope and determination. The time had come to fight for her marriage. She was ready. Even if it meant tying Merrick to the bed, which was exactly why she stood in the bedroom of their suite with two silk scarves.

Could she possibly be so bold as to force her husband to submit to her desires? Would he even want to? His aggressive and dominant nature would probably balk at the idea. Only one way to find out.

Chloe placed the makeshift binding on the nightstand next to the wine chilling in the ice bucket. She went to the bathroom and checked her appearance one more time. She'd gone shopping early in the day at the little boutique attached to the hotel and bought herself a sexy, red, pleated babydoll and matching thong panties set. She didn't bother with makeup other than a little pink lip gloss, and she'd left her hair down, just the way Merrick liked it.

She'd managed to get him out of the suite when she'd explained she had a surprise that would make their last night special. He'd grumbled a little, but she could see the anticipation in the blue depths of his eyes, too.

Chloe heard the card key in the lock, and her stomach bottomed out. Oh, God. Showtime.

She walked back into the bedroom and picked up the silk scarf, then waited for her husband to enter the room. She didn't wait long. Merrick suddenly stood in the doorway, fists clenched at his sides, nostrils flaring. He looked her over with slow purpose, taking her in from head to toe. She could swear her knees knocked together.

"You take my breath away."

The deep timbre of his voice floated over her, sending her into a new realm. It fueled her courage as nothing else could. "Thank you, Merrick."

He moved across the room and stopped inches from her. He reached out, grasped the spaghetti strap of her negligee and played with it. "This is new."

"Yeah, I bought it earlier today." Jesus, was that her voice? It sounded as if she'd swallowed a mouthful of sand.

He peered over her shoulder, then back at her. "Wine?"

Chloe held up the scarf. "And silk."

He frowned. "For what?"

"Your hands."

His brows shot up so high, she almost burst out laughing. "You want to tie me up?"

"Yes. I want you to let me take control tonight. Think you can handle that?"

Merrick leaned closer. She could feel his hot breath against her lips, see the heat in his eyes. "I can handle anything you can dish out, baby."

Yeah, okay, that had her panties growing damp. Chloe knew a challenge when she heard one, and Merrick had just tossed down the gauntlet.

She smoothed the scarf between her palms, drawing her husband's attention to the colorful bit of material. "How about you get undressed."

Merrick's sexy grin lit her up like a brush fire. "Yes, ma'am," he complied in a fake Texas drawl.

Chloe turned around and poured two glasses of wine, then picked one up, took a sip and then another. When she placed the wineglass back on the nightstand and turned, Merrick was fully nude and grinning like the cat that swallowed the canary.

Her husband had always made her drool, but tonight he had a different sort of gleam in eyes. Something she'd never seen there before. His hard cock seemed bigger than ever. She licked her lips and counted to ten.

"Lie down on the bed, in the center," she directed. Merrick winked and sat, before moving to the middle of the bed. He stretched out, flung his arms behind his head, and crossed his legs at the ankles. He didn't speak at all, which created a new sort of nervous tension in her.

Chloe knelt on the bed and held out the scarf. She dangled it above his abs. "I plan to make this night unforgettable."

"It is already, baby."

Chloe laughed. "I haven't even done anything yet!"

Merrick reached out and flicked his thumb over one satin covered nipple. "Just looking at you is enough to have me embarrassing myself right now." He pinched the turgid peak, and her pussy throbbed. "Mmm, I just love red."

"It's your favorite color."

"Yes. Do you know why?"

"No, why?"

"You had a red blouse on the day you came in for the interview. A red blouse and a black skirt. Christ, I wanted to push that skirt up and fuck you against the desk. It was hard as hell keeping my hands off you."

Chloe couldn't believe her ears. "You remember what I wore?" Heck, she didn't even remember! "That was over two years ago."

"I'll never forget it," he swore. "You turned me inside out that day. You were always the one. Always."

Warmth filled her. "Whenever I think I couldn't possibly love you more, you say something like that and I fall all over again."

"And I intend to keep saying them. I never want you to forget how much you mean to me."

It was easy for Merrick to make the declaration, because work wasn't breathing down his neck at the moment. What would happen when they got back home and work beckoned once again? By sheer will, Chloe drove those thoughts out of her mind. She didn't want to go there, not tonight. Tonight she would seduce her husband.

"Put your wrists together."

Merrick didn't say a word as he brought both arms over his torso and crossed one hand over the other. Chloe inched closer and wrapped the scarf around her husband's thick, tan wrists. She tied it in a knot and sat back, gauging his reaction.

Merrick flung his arms over his head and spoke in a low tone. "Come and get it, angel."

"Oh, I intend to," she purred. Chloe crawled on top of Merrick, straddling him. Placing both hands on his chest, she sifted her fingers through the dark, soft curls. His muscles jumped. The feel of his cock nestled beneath her bottom added an extra level of stimulation. Keeping her eyes on his, she leaned down and licked his nipple. Merrick's lips thinned, his gaze burning with need. Chloe luxuriated in his undivided attention. Feminine power flowed through her as she embraced a side of her nature she'd never known existed.

"Bite it, Chloe. Show me who's boss."

Merrick's words were so incongruent to the man she knew him to be. Her dominant, sometimes uncivilized, husband was pushing her to take charge. "I've never known this side of you," she mused.

"And I've never known you to want to be in control. Sometimes stepping outside our cozy box is not just fun, but necessary."

He was right. "I guess I'm stepping out of the box then," she surmised.

Merrick winked. "Hell, you didn't step out, you jumped out. I'm yours. You can do anything you want to me right now. So, what do you want, angel?"

"For starters, I need to taste you," she answered. She lowered over him and melded their lips together. Merrick shuddered beneath her touch. He lifted his head, smashing his lips against hers. Chloe licked his fuller bottom lip, and Merrick's arms slowly came around her head, caging her in. Even tied he figured out a way to take control of their pleasure. When his mouth opened and his tongue played with hers, Chloe forgot how things were supposed to go. All she cared about, all she needed, was his touch, his lips, his tongue. Him.

He sucked her tongue into his mouth and growled, the sound reverberating clear to her womb. His mouth devoured hers. He pushed and nipped at her lips, forcing her to open for him, to give him access to a place no other had a right to enter. Chloe had never experienced a kiss quite like Merrick's. He knew how much pressure to add, how rough his little love bites should be. His kisses could make her come. He'd always been as potent as a drug. As addicting as chocolate, and just as lethal as a hungry panther. Other men couldn't compare to Merrick.

Chloe trembled as he licked and scoured her mouth, insisting on tasting every spot, branding her with his unique flavor. His arms around her head held her still for his plundering, and Chloe helplessly surrendered everything in that moment. His lips were almost brutal in his assault.

He lifted an inch. "You make me ache. I fucking ache for you, baby." Chloe moaned his name, her body wild for his touches. This time when he kissed her, he wasn't asking for entrance, he expected it. She melted and opened, then promptly went up in flames.

Chloe dug her fingers into his hair. God, she loved his hair, so thick and full. She let her fingers delve and grab handfuls of the dark silk. Merrick pulled his lips away and groaned her name. She sensed a change in him. He'd had enough of letting her take the lead. He'd be wrenching the reins back if she didn't do something.

"Please, let me play," she softly pleaded. "Just a moment longer."

Merrick's gaze bored into her, as if seeing into her very core. "I can't deny you, you know I can't."

"You won't regret it," she promised.

Merrick pulled his arms away, releasing her. "Play with me, angel."

Chapter Eleven

If he kept from shooting his load early, it'd be a goddamn miracle. Seeing Chloe in the little red nightie had shredded his self-control. The instant she'd wrapped the silk around his wrists, his balls had drawn up tight. She wanted to be the one in control. He was only too happy to oblige. Afterwards, it'd be his turn.

"I bought more than wine and lingerie today."

What did the minx have up her sleeve now? "Oh, yeah?"

Chloe reached toward the nightstand and opened the drawer. She pulled out a small plastic bottle and held it above him. He inspected the label in the dimly lit room. His lips quirked. "You want to give me a massage?"

"Sort of," she answered vaguely. Her voice drifted over him, as soft as the satin she wore and twice as lethal.

Chloe's warm brown eyes overwhelmed his senses and left him panting like a little lost pup. He'd be begging to get inside her tight, hot cunt in a few more seconds; he could feel it in his bones. She owned him, body and soul. Her dainty fingers drifted over his torso, and he shuddered. She could tear him apart with barely a stroke of her sharp fingernail. That wasn't anything new, though. Chloe always held power over him. She didn't realize how easily she could control him. He'd always been careful to keep that knowledge from her. Now he knew he'd made a mistake in not letting down his guard. If she understood how much he craved her, how he'd shrivel and die without her, she'd know he was sincere about making their marriage work. She'd know he meant to keep her, to have babies with her, to put her before work.

Chloe removed the lid on the bottle and squirted some of the sweet smelling liquid onto her hands. As she rubbed them together, Merrick took in the sight of her sitting astride him. Her nipples were hard little points covered in the softest satin he'd ever seen. His mouth watered as he anticipated licking and suckling. Her damp pussy against his crotch had him so hard he could crack cement. Each time she wiggled, he ached a little more. The need to slam inside her tight heat nearly overrode everything else.

As her hands began to stroke his torso, he bit down hard on the urge to force her hands lower. He wanted to feel that slippery glide up and down the rigid length of his dick, feel her small hands squeezing and playing with his hot flesh.

"Lower, Chloe," he snarled as he flexed his hands. The silk was about to be torn in two if she didn't move a little faster.

"I want to touch, to tease. You wouldn't deny me, would you, Merrick?"

"I can't take much more of this slow seduction, baby. I'm about to explode."

Chloe laughed. The lilting sound tore a growl from his chest. "I swear, you're so impatient."

"Touch my cock," he softly demanded. "Just once. Give me something to hold me over."

Chloe's fingers slid lower, down the muscles of his abdomen, then over one hip. The little seductress bypassed his groin altogether. He pushed his hips upward, hard, nearly unseating her, only slightly mollified by her sharp cry of surprise.

"Touch my cock, or the game's over," he warned.

Her eyes widened. "What are you saying?"

"I'm saying I'm about to rip this cute little scarf,"—he wiggled his wrists for emphasis—"and throw you on your stomach so I can plow into your soft little body. Nice and hard, just the way you like it."

Even with the room dimly lit, Merrick could see the blush that stole over his wife's face. She bit her lip and shimmied down his body until she was perched on top of his thighs. She grasped his heavy cock in both hands and squeezed. Merrick grabbed the headboard and clamped down on the need to take over. Her fingers drifted up and down, her little pinky sliding over the slit in the engorged head, playing and drawing a bead of moisture to the tip. She swiped it up and brought it to her mouth. Merrick watched in fascination as she closed her eyes and sucked on her pinky. Her sweet moans of pleasure rippled clear through to his soul, heating his blood.

"God, baby, you look like sin. A tempting little girl playing with fire."

Chloe opened her eyes and leaned down. Her hot breath against his ear fueled his already out of control need to take her. "I'm not a little girl though, am I, Merrick? I'm a grown woman and I know exactly what I want." She nipped his earlobe for emphasis before sliding her palm over his cock and ball sac.

The last thread of his control snapped at the same time that the threads on the scarf tore.

Merrick had her beneath him in between one heartbeat, and the next, his hands framing her face. "You go to my head, baby. I can't breathe, can't think. All I want is you. Your cunt, your ass, your mouth. I want to slide inside you and stay there. I want to fuck you so hard you'll never walk away from me again. I want to make you ache and scream so you'll pour that sweet juice all over my dick."

Chloe arched upward and shouted, "Oh, Merrick, please!"

"Shh, it's time for me to play," he crooned. He grasped both her hands in one of his and pulled them above her head, putting her on display for his viewing pleasure alone. His entire body vibrated with repressed rage as he imagined her finding someone else. No way in hell. No other man would ever see her like this, he silently vowed. No other would ever touch what belonged to him. He had the crazy urge to mark her, to prove to them both that no one else would ever do for either of them.

Merrick's lips crashed down on hers. The kiss was hard and greedy, demanding entrance to her mouth. She whimpered and opened for him. His tongue thrust in and out as he licked and fucked her hot, tempting mouth. He nipped her lower lip, swiped his tongue over the small sting, before drifting lower. He dropped kisses along her chin and tasted the length of her neck, sucking and sipping at her feminine perfection. Merrick moved lower, pushed the straps of her nightie off her shoulders, and bit down, eliciting a moan of carnal pleasure from his gentle wife.

Merrick pulled back and tugged the pretty red satin over her head, exposing her round breasts and nipped-in waist. He tossed it to the floor before moving his attention to the minuscule panties. His fingers shook as he pulled the material down her hips. Every muscle in his body went still at the erotic sight that greeted him.

"Oh, fuck, baby."

"D-Do you like it?"

Merrick couldn't stop staring. His wife, the woman who'd stolen his heart with barely a whisper, had waxed her pussy bare. Nothing but smooth, creamy skin and slick moisture greeted his insatiable gaze. He licked his lips and touched her exposed clit with his thumb, rasping over the little button with teasing strokes. Chloe moaned and moved against him. His nostrils flared as he took in the scent of her arousal. Holy hell. And he'd thought he couldn't get any harder? He'd be lucky to keep from coming all over the bed!

"You've been a very busy girl, baby," Merrick murmured as he fingered her creamy slit.

"I hoped you'd be pleased," she whispered as she ground against his palm.

"Mmm, I'm very pleased. You look fucking delicious and Daddy's mighty hungry." He wedged his shoulders between her thighs, pushing her legs apart, and filled his palms with the sweet globes of her ass. Merrick skipped the preliminaries and simply dove in, sliding his tongue deep, tasting her hot channel and creamy desire. Chloe's fingers tunneled into his hair as she pushed him against her further, forcing his tongue deeper. He let loose a low moan, knowing she'd feel the vibration over her sensitive clit and pussy. He flicked her little nub several times, then watched as Chloe flung her head back and screamed out her climax, drenching him in liquid desire.

He kissed and teased until he'd wrung every last drop from her. She collapsed backward, her hands falling to the mattress. Merrick lifted to his knees and grabbed two pillows. He lifted her hips and pushed the pillows beneath her, propping up her lower body. Chloe never budged. He grabbed the wine bottle and pulled it out of the ice bucket, then set it aside. As he brought the bucket of ice to the bed, Merrick reached in and grabbed a slippery cube. He slid it over Chloe's left nipple. She yelped.

"Damn it, Merrick, that's cold!"

Merrick chuckled as he watched angry sparks flashing in

Chloe's eyes. "Awake, are we?"

"Yes," she gritted out.

"Good. I would hate for you to miss this," he murmured as he touched her other nipple with the slick ice. Chloe gasped and tried to push his hand away, but he wasn't about to let her. "Put your hands on the headboard, baby."

"Drop the ice and I will."

"Hmm, that sounds like an ultimatum, angel," Merrick murmured as he grabbed Chloe's wrists and held them above her head. "You know how much I love a challenge."

He stroked the ice between her succulent tits, mesmerized by the little jiggle as she squirmed and pleaded with him to drop the ice.

"Relax, baby," he softly urged. "Just close your eyes and feel."

As he moved lower, over her slightly rounded belly, Merrick felt Chloe begin to relax her hands. He released them slowly, but kept his gaze on her face as he drew the rapidly melting cube over her freshly shaved mound. Chloe's breath caught, but she didn't push him away. Merrick tossed the cube away and drew another from the metal bucket. He hovered just above her clit and ordered, "Hands on the headboard. Now." This time, she didn't hesitate. Her elegant fingers wrapped around the top of the bed. Merrick had a wild urge to howl at the moon as he stared down at his wife. With her kiss-swollen lips parted, her brown eyes filled with anticipation as she watched his every move, Merrick knew he'd found heaven.

As gentle as he was capable of being in that moment, Merrick stroked Chloe's clit with the cold cube. Her body bowed, and his cock throbbed at the erotic sight. He slid it back and forth, then dipped between her swollen folds. Chloe's hips shot upward.

"Oh, God, what are you doing to me?"

"Fucking my pretty little wife," he ground out as he drew the small chip up and down, but the heat of her cunt melted the fragile cube too quickly. He grabbed another cube and smoothed it around her clit, eliciting several moans of approval from Chloe, her hips gyrating in her need for release. Merrick drew the ice down her slit to the pink pucker of her ass. He rimmed the small opening, his mouth watering as he imagined licking her there, fucking her. Hard and fast and deep, so deep their souls would fuse together.

"Merrick!" Chloe shouted.

Merrick detected the slightest note of uneasiness in her voice, as if fighting against the pleasure of having him in such a forbidden place. "Hush, baby, let me play."

He swirled the cube over her tight little ass several more times as she squirmed and called his name, her need mounting higher, burning hotter. As Merrick drew the cube over her scorching skin, he watched in fascination as it finally turned to liquid. He placed the ice bucket back on the nightstand and grabbed the bottle of oil Chloe had used on him earlier. He popped the top and soaked his fingers with the sweet smelling fluid. He sat back on his haunches and slid his fingers over her wet anus. Chloe's eyes shot wide, her face flushed with arousal.

"You want me here, baby?" Merrick asked as he slid one finger inside her tight little ass. It was barely an inch and already she writhed and moaned. In the two years they'd been married, they'd never had anal sex. He'd always held that part of his nature away from her. He'd wanted to be gentle with Chloe. Civilized. Now he knew he'd been wrong in holding back.

Merrick slid in another inch. "Tell me," he coaxed. "You want this hot little ass fucked? You're going to have to ask me nicely."

"I-I don't know."

Merrick let another finger join the first, stretching her, preparing her for the invasion of his cock. "Yes, you do. Don't be afraid, baby."

"Will it hurt?"

He could hear the fear in her voice, but also desire. Merrick wiggled his fingers deeper. She moaned. "It'll be tight and we'll have to take it slow, but I'd never hurt you, angel. Never."

Chloe's gaze met his, and Merrick knew she was on fire. Aching and hurting. They both needed this. He pulled his fingers free. Chloe pleaded with him, begging him to fill her again. This time when he slid the two digits in, he buried them deep. He pumped several times and Chloe pushed against him, fucking his fingers. "Answer me, damn it. I need to fuck you, Chloe. I'm about to go up in flames here. Do I take your pussy or your ass? Which is it to be?"

"Please, fuck my ass, Merrick!"

Merrick slipped his fingers free and grabbed the bottle of oil again. He squirted the slippery fluid onto his cock, readying himself for the clutch of Chloe's body. He went to his knees and wrapped his fist around his engorged length, then stroked the bulbous head over her sweet little pucker. Chloe gasped and bit her lip, still clutching the headboard. Merrick slipped inside, barely over the rim.

"Holy hell, you're tight," he ground out. "The tightest little fist holding my cock prisoner." As he tried to push in an inch more, he was forced to stop. "Chloe, baby, you're not relaxing. Don't tense up on me."

"I-I can't help it."

Merrick stretched out on top of her, bracing his arms on either side of her head, and kissed her with gentle reverence. His lips played with hers, sipping at her sweetness. Her arms came around his shoulders and her legs wrapped around his hips as she surrendered to him completely. He felt her inner muscles relax and took advantage, pushing all the way in, filling her with his hard cock.

"Chloe, sweet Chloe," he mouthed against her lips. She pushed her tongue into his mouth and lifted her hips, forcing his cock deeper still, his balls cushioned against her ass cheeks.

In the soft cradle of Chloe's body, Merrick had found his paradise.

Chapter Twelve

Chloe stared up at her husband's feral expression, captivated by the change in him. He'd always been gentle and sweet in his loving. Looking at him now, it was as if he'd opened a door to his soul and let a wild man out of its cage. She'd known he could be rough and aggressive, but he'd never shown her that part of his nature. Until now. It frightened her a little, but it also turned her on. Her husband was giving her something special, his complete self. No walls, no holding back. Just Merrick at his most primal.

"Your eyes are devouring me, babe," he whispered as his fingers coasted down her side and over to her mound to play with her clit. Chloe's pussy clenched as the pleasure spiked anew. "Do you like having my cock inside this ass?"

"Yes," she breathed out, "it feels so good. Every time you move, I can feel every little pulse from your cock."

He thrust his hips forward, his heavy length stroking nerve endings she'd never known existed. With each erotic glide, he grew more frantic. His fingers flicked and toyed with her clitoris. Chloe's blood surged in her veins. Her legs clamped tighter around his hips in an effort to bring them both to that pinnacle of rapture.

"You're going to crave it," he vowed. "We'll both crave it."

Chloe moaned and writhed as Merrick fucked her ass and

pumped her clit. He surrounded her with his powerful body and wild hunger.

Merrick wrapped a fist in her hair and forced her to look at him. "This ass is for me. No other, Chloe. Your pussy, your mouth, it's all mine. I'll never let you go."

Chloe tried to shake her head, to deny his words. To insert some of her own dominance. He would have none of it. He pulled out of her, then thrust in again, hard and deep. His fingers played with her little nub with expert skill. A pinch, a stroke. He knew how high to take her before letting her come back down, only to do it all over again. Working her body as if he knew it better than she.

"Merrick, please!"

"You want to come, baby?"

"You know I do!" Chloe cried as she gripped his shoulders, her nails biting into flesh and muscle.

"Admit the truth and I'll give you what you need," he softly urged. "Admit we belong together. Let me hear you say the words."

He wanted her to surrender, body and soul. To give her trust to him. She didn't dare. Not when things were still so uncertain between them. "I can't give you that, Merrick."

Merrick pulled out of her completely, leaving her bereft. Within seconds he had her on her stomach, her bottom raised in the air from the pillows he'd placed beneath her earlier. He leaned down and whispered against the shell of her ear. "Say it," he demanded. "You're mine. I'm yours."

She tried to sit up, but his palm on her back held her prisoner. "Be still and give me what I want."

"This can't be settled like this. It's not that simple."

"It is that simple," he snarled. His palm coasted down her

back, then over her buttocks. Chloe squirmed beneath his touch. Fire licked up her spine. She needed him to fill her, to take them both to that place only he seemed able to find.

"Give it to me, baby. I'll make you scream with pleasure. All you have to do is be a good girl and say the words."

"No," she ground out, tempting the beast.

Her only warning that she'd pushed too far was a sudden gust of air that snaked over her bottom seconds before his palm connected with her sensitive flesh. He'd spanked her! "How dare you!"

"Say it."

She tried to break free, but he only held her down with one hand and swatted her again. This time the other cheek. Her flesh stung. Two more swats and Chloe no longer wanted up. Her body was a blazing inferno of need. Her pussy throbbed, and juices dripped down her thighs. Merrick petted her, soothing the ache. "Will you say the words?"

"This isn't fair. You know it isn't. Please, Merrick."

"I don't have the luxury to play fair. The gloves came off the instant you left me."

Chloe heard the pain in his voice. She'd done that. She'd made him hurt. It had never been her intention. She'd only needed her husband back.

Merrick stretched out on top of her and used his knee to push her legs apart. When the head of his cock touched her anus, she moaned. Merrick pushed inside. One slow, torturous inch at a time until finally he'd filled her completely. He kissed her neck and murmured sweet words of love while he pumped against her. His fingers sought out her clit again, only this time he didn't stop his sweet torment until she'd reached that delicious crest again. Her body tightened as waves of pleasure threw her into another realm. She screamed his name as bursts of rapture splintered her mind.

Merrick went wild, driving into her, grinding his cock deep. With his arms surrounding her, caging her in, keeping her beneath him, he gave his passion free rein.

Chloe flexed her muscles, dragging a curse from Merrick. "Chloe! Oh, hell, baby," he groaned, his voice strangled with emotion and desire. Three more hard thrusts and he erupted. Hot jets of come filled her ass.

He collapsed on top of her, both of them exhausted and sweating. Chloe thought it was the most wonderful feeling in the world to have her husband's big, hard body wrapped around her, cock still seated deep. She never wanted the moment to end.

"I spanked you."

Chloe's face heated. "Yes, you did."

Merrick lifted away, pulling out. Already she missed the connection. He turned her over and took her chin in his palm, forcing her to look at him. "You liked it."

"Maybe."

Merrick grinned. "No maybes, baby. You liked it when I smacked that pretty little ass."

Suddenly Chloe was reminded of the pain on Merrick's face when he'd mentioned her leaving him. Tears came to her eyes as she came to know the truth. She'd deserted him, giving up on their marriage. She'd walked out, and it had hurt him.

"Baby?" Merrick's voice, so filled with concern, only caused her to cry more. "Ah, hell, I'm sorry. I never should have spanked you. I'm sorry, baby, don't cry. Please don't cry."

Chloe shook her head as she realized he'd misunderstood. "It's not that," she said as the tears came in a rush. "You were right, I did like it."

Merrick stared at her a few seconds before leaning down and kissing the tears away. "I love you, Chloe."

"I love you, too, so much."

Merrick didn't say anything else as he pulled her into his arms and started toward the bathroom. He stood her on her feet and turned on the shower. Once he had the temperature just right, he stepped inside and brought her with him. They were both quiet as the heat surrounded them. She settled against his chest and let the world slip away. For a few minutes they just stood there, Merrick stroking her hair, kissing her cheeks, her holding him close, inhaling his intoxicating male scent.

"Talk to me, angel. Let me in," he crooned.

"I hurt you. When I left, I hurt you."

He pulled back and stared down into her face. "That's what the tears were about?"

Shame had her hiding her face again. She didn't want him looking at her when she admitted the awful truth. With her nose pressed against his chest, she muttered, "I gave up on us. I shouldn't have given up."

"Aww, baby, you never gave up, not really. You were just helping me get my head on straight."

"It's been so hard these last months. I never wanted to walk out. I never wanted that for us."

"I know. And as much as I hate to admit it, I think it was the right move."

Her gaze shot to his. "You mean that?"

He slid his hands over her shoulders, then on down to cup her ass. "I've been such a fool. I figured if I kept busy with work, I wouldn't have to think too hard about what had me all mixed up inside. I wouldn't have to deal with it. All I did was make things worse."

Chloe sifted her fingers through Merrick's wet hair. "I don't know where we go from here."

"Come back," he asserted. "That's the only way I can prove to you that I have my priorities in order."

Chloe stayed quiet, her mind in chaos as she contemplated her options. How was she to know he wouldn't go right back to his crazy schedule the minute the plane landed? She still needed time. Nothing was really settled. "I can't come home. Not yet. I'm sorry, but I just can't."

Merrick's hold on her tightened. "I swear it'll be different, baby. You have my word. I'm going to have Jackson take up some of my after-hours responsibilities. I can't ever promise it'll be nine to five. I own the company, after all, but I can promise it won't be 'round the clock the way it has been, not anymore."

She cupped the back of his head and said, "I never expected nine to five. I knew what I was getting into when we married."

"Then come home."

"I love you. When I think about a future without you, my stomach hurts and I feel like someone's stabbing me in the chest." She took a deep breath then let it out. "Please understand. I'm not giving up on us, but I'm not convinced anything will change. Right now you're trying to win me back, but how do I know that feeling won't change the minute your cell phone goes off and there's some new social event you have to attend or some crisis that requires your attention?"

A muscle in his jaw jumped. "You don't, but I'll prove I'm serious about this. You'll see for yourself. I love you, too, wife. Nothing else matters."

She bit her lip and looked away as she remembered her plan to find a new job. "I was going to quit," she admitted. "I even updated my resume."

He tugged on her chin, forcing her to look at him. "If you won't move back in, at least keep your job. That's the only way you'll be able to see with your own eyes that I'm serious about making some changes."

He was right. If she stayed at Vaughn's then at least she'd know for herself if his new mantra would stick. Plus, she'd get to see him on a daily basis. "Okay, I'll stay."

He smiled and stroked her chin. "Good," he murmured. "In the meantime, we still have the suite until morning and I want to make love to my wife again."

His head descended, and Chloe surrendered. The kiss was hard and filled with possessive heat. Oh, God, how would she ever have the strength to stick to her guns? He was much too addicting. It was just that simple.

♦

Merrick was going slowly insane. It'd been a full week since they'd returned from Hawaii and Chloe had stayed true to her word. While she kept working at Vaughn's, she'd moved out of the hotel and into her dad's house. It'd been hell trying to sleep without her. He was running on pure fear alone. Fear that she may never come back to him. Every morning he saw her at her desk was like a living hell, but not seeing her would have been worse. It was small consolation to know she wasn't giving up on him entirely.

"Hey, you in there?"

Jackson's voice jerked him back to the task at hand. It was late afternoon on Friday and Merrick had pulled his V.P. off a project so they could discuss the changes he'd been contemplating ever since Chloe had moved out. "As I was saying

I need to cut back on my hours. That's where you come in."

"I'm all ears."

"The biggest problem seems to be the social events and the local commerce meetings. Also the Multiple Sclerosis charity that Vaughn's sponsors. I'd like you to take over these events."

Jackson nodded. "Works for me."

Merrick thought for a second, then said, "Also, I want you to interview someone for the sales rep position."

"You have someone in mind?"

"My cousin Grace. She's been pestering me about hiring her. She's just graduated with her bachelor's, and I'd like you to do the interview."

Jackson surprised him when he frowned and sat back in his chair. "Does she know I'm doing the interview?"

He shook his head. Merrick knew Jackson and Grace butted heads on occasion, but he'd never understood why. "No. I haven't talked to her yet. Is there a problem?"

"Nope, none at all. I'll set it up immediately."

"Let me run it by her first," Merrick said. He hoped Grace wouldn't give him a hard time about Jackson doing the interview, but he had a feeling she would. He should delve deeper, find out what it was with the two of them, but he didn't really have it in him to give a damn. All he could concentrate on was Chloe. The door to his office opened and she appeared, as if his thoughts had conjured her.

She walked across the room and handed him some documents. "I need your signature on these."

Merrick took them and turned to Jackson. "I'll send you a schedule of upcoming events."

Jackson stood. "Sounds good."

After he left, Merrick's gaze zeroed in on Chloe. Damn she

looked good. The black slacks and emerald green blouse she wore hugged a body he longed to touch. "How's it going with your dad?"

She smiled and tucked a stray lock of hair behind her ear. "It's okay. We stay out of each other's way for the most part."

"I miss you, baby," Merrick said, unable to contain it much longer. He'd wanted to give her room, but, damn, he was getting desperate.

She blushed and looked down at the floor. "I miss you, too."

Merrick stood and moved around the desk. When he was within touching distance, he murmured, "I promised not to push and I intended to keep my word. I just want you to know that things are in motion. I've already talked to Jackson."

Chloe looked up, her hungry gaze eating him alive. "I heard you two talking when I came in."

Unable to resist, he reached out and stroked her cheek with his thumb. "My bed is cold without you. I haven't slept more than an hour a night."

"Me, either," she said, her soft voice caressing his senses. "And I think I'm keeping Dad up with my restlessness."

Merrick smoothed his thumb down her cheek to her lips. God, he wanted to taste her. "There's a solution, you know," he whispered, emotion clogging his throat.

"Merrick—"

He stopped her with a kiss, unable to bear another denial. He kept it brief, all too aware they were at the office. "I won't give up on you, baby," he vowed against her lips.

"I wouldn't want you to," she murmured. She cupped his cheek in her palm and smiled. "Merrick Vaughn is no quitter."

He winked and dropped his hands. "Damn straight." When she moved away, putting distance between them, Merrick blurted, "Come over tonight. For dinner, nothing more."

She squinted at him suspiciously. "You'll try to seduce me."

He shook his head and tucked his hands into his front pockets. "Just dinner, baby. I'll order Chinese or something."

She was quiet for a moment and Merrick was afraid she would deny him. Finally, she smiled. "What time?"

"Seven. Does that work?"

She nodded. "Want me to bring anything?"

"Just an appetite. I'll take care of the rest."

"Okay. I'll see you tonight."

Merrick watched her leave. His heartbeat had sped up, and his mind was already envisioning the night ahead. It was too early to bust out the champagne, but at least he wouldn't be eating alone again. He'd have Chloe all to himself for a few hours. It was something.

◆

Chloe shifted on the soft white rug in front of the fireplace and adjusted the spaghetti straps of the lacy red teddy she'd bought earlier in the day. She imagined Merrick walking into their home and finding her displayed like a present wrapped in satin. Her temperature spiked and her pussy grew damp. Damn, she hadn't been this excited since their honeymoon night.

The minute she'd overheard Merrick handing over his social duties to Jackson, she'd known she wouldn't be spending another night at her dad's house. Merrick's dinner offer had provided the perfect opportunity to surprise him. But a simple dinner wouldn't do. She didn't want to come home and quietly fall back into their life together, she wanted a fresh start. An exciting start.

He'd promised to make some changes, and she'd seen first hand that he was a man of his word. He hadn't given up on their marriage and it was time she proved she wasn't about to either. When she heard the whir of the automatic garage door, her stomach did a little flip-flop. She heard the door open then close. Suddenly Merrick was there, staring at her, the bag of food and bottle of wine clearly forgotten.

"Jesus," he groaned as he looked her over.

Chloe smiled, recognizing the arousal heating his blue eyes. She held her hands out to her sides and asked, "Do you like it?"

He placed the food and wine on the counter, then strode across the room. He fell to his knees in front of her and touched one lace-covered breast. "You look amazing. Damn, baby."

Her body came alive at his words, and his light caress sent fire licking through her veins. "I wanted to surprise you."

He pulled back and Chloe missed his touch immediately. "What does this mean?"

"It means I want to come home," she declared. "I want to start over. It means I love you, through the good times and the bad."

Merrick grabbed her around the waist and pulled her onto his lap. He buried his head in her hair. "Fuck, I've missed you. Don't ever leave me again. Never again, baby."

Chloe wrapped her arms around his head and held him tight. She could feel his body trembling. Tears sprang to her eyes. "No, never again. I promise."

He lifted his head and crushed his mouth to hers. He was hard, rough, forcing her lips apart and sweeping his tongue inside, teasing her into a frenzy of need. He tasted of spice and hot, aroused man, and Chloe would always crave his wild flavor.

Merrick pulled back before cupping her cheeks in his large, calloused palms. "I love you. This week has been pure hell."

"I wanted to come home so badly, please understand. I needed to see for myself, Merrick."

"Shh," he soothed, "I know, it's okay."

Letting her fingers drift through his soft dark hair, Chloe said, "I do want one thing from you."

"Anything, sweetheart. Just name it."

"I want us to go to marriage counseling." When he frowned, she knew he hated the idea of an outsider getting into their personal affairs, but she also knew they needed help, so she stayed firm. "It's important to me."

"What could a shrink do that we can't do on our own?"

She shrugged. "Maybe nothing. Maybe it won't be necessary. But I want you to at least consider the idea." When it was clear he was still going to argue, she barreled on. "You have some unresolved issues. You admitted it yourself. It could help to talk to someone. We'll do it together."

He gritted his teeth. She could see the muscle jumping in his jaw. It went against his nature to admit to failure. When he sighed, she knew the truth before he spoke. And she loved him all the more for it.

"If it's what you want, if it gets you back in my bed where you damn well belong, then we'll go to marriage counseling."

She pressed against him and placed a gentle kiss to his lips. Merrick crushed her to his chest, his hands cupping her ass, fitting their bodies together. Chloe pulled back an inch and, with emotion clogging her throat, whispered, "I love you, for now and for always."

Merrick's blue eyes heated, darkened. "I love you, too, baby. There will never be another who fills me the way you do. You give me strength. You make me want to be a better man. You make me feel ten feet tall. As God is my witness, with you I know I can do anything."

"Even fatherhood?" she hedged.

Merrick's lips quirked into an ornery grin. "Definitely. In fact, I think we should get started immediately."

Her heart soared. "Really?"

"Hell, yeah. I'm already imagining you barefoot and pregnant."

"Don't go all Neanderthal on me, big guy. I'm *so* not June Cleaver."

"Fine, then, just pregnant," he acquiesced. "But first let me unwrap my pretty present."

"Definitely," she groaned.

He tugged the straps of her teddy down her shoulders and her breasts sprang free. He licked his lips. "Mmm, so sweet."

His mouth covered one hard nipple, and Chloe surrendered to her husband's touch.

Epilogue

"You're such a dork, Merrick! Stop fiddling with it and let me see it."

"Lacey, I can cook a friggin' hamburger, it's not that hard."

"You're squishing all the juice out!"

Merrick pointed the metal spatula over Lacey's shoulder. "Nick, will you please find your wife something to do? She's driving me nuts."

Nick laughed and wrapped his right arm around Lacey's middle, drawing a frown from Merrick. It still seemed strange to see his best friend and his little sister together. He wondered if he'd ever get used to it. Thankfully, they'd finally tied the knot. They'd kept it simple and small. No frills, like Lacey. There'd been a collective family sigh of relief when Lacey had walked down the aisle at last.

"I've got just the thing," Nick murmured. "Come on, baby. Let Merrick burn the food."

Lacey harrumphed even as she allowed Nick to pull her away. Merrick *so* didn't want to know what Nick had in mind for Lacey.

"I think you're doing a terrific job."

Merrick swung around. His breath caught. At three weeks pregnant, nothing had changed about his wife's body. But the knowledge that she carried his child sent a dose of pure male pride through him.

Merrick crooked his finger. "Come here, give me a kiss."

Chloe closed the gap separating them. In an instant, Merrick had her in his arms, his mouth slanted over hers. He sucked at her lips, teasing his way into her mouth. She tasted like apple juice. Sweet and tangy. He wanted to sip at her all day. He lifted an inch and whispered, "Daddy's hungry, angel."

"Mmm, yes," she sighed, "but we'll have to wait until after the barbeque."

Merrick ground his teeth together. Damn, their family get-togethers always went late into the evening. "I have a treat for you," he tempted her.

Chloe pulled back, her eyes alight with excitement. "You do?"

"Yeah." He leaned close and whispered, "I bought you a paddle."

Chloe gasped. "Merrick!"

"Figure out a way to leave early and I'll give you a pretty red ass as a reward."

"You're insatiable," she replied, but he noticed she didn't seem too upset by that fact.

He winked. "And you love it."

"Love what?"

Merrick knew that voice. He mentally counted to ten and turned around. His cousin, Grace Vaughn, followed by a pissed off Blade. At five foot three inches and one hundred and ten pounds, Grace was trouble with a capital T. "None of your business, brat."

"Aw, that's no fun."

"Why aren't you in the house torturing Blade?"

"He lost. Three times. I swear he's a spoilsport, too."

"Chess or poker?"

Grace grinned like the imp she was. "Chess, and I got forty dollars out of that big lug."

Merrick quirked a brow at Blade. "You actually bet money? Thought you were smarter than that, bro." No one placed bets against Grace. She was the best damn chess player around. She'd competed in college and still had a reputation.

"Hell, I would have won, but she brought out the timer," Blade complained. "I hate that stupid timer.

Grace laughed and patted Blade on the arm. "It's that Vaughn male pride. Gets you boys every time."

"Maybe you're just not playing with the right guy."

Grace flushed and swiveled on her heel. "And you'd be the right guy, huh?"

Jackson stood to Grace's left, his eyes filled with challenge. What the hell?

"I think I could definitely give you a run for your money, little girl."

She snorted and planted her hand on her hip. "You wish."

Jackson crossed his arms over his chest. "Afraid I'll win?"

Grace mimicked his pose, then stuck her nose in the air. "Afraid you'll cry like a baby when you lose."

Blade chuckled. "Be careful, Jackson. I'm convinced Grace sold her soul to the devil to play chess as well as she does."

Candice walked up and wrapped an arm around Blade's waist, which resulted in Blade hauling Candice off to the side of the house and behind some bushes. Lucky bastard. Merrick wanted to haul Chloe off. He would have too had his mother not suckered him into manning the grill.

Jackson's disgruntled tone as he remarked about a blonde devil in blue jeans pulled Merrick away from Blade and Candice's naughty rendezvous. As his gaze caught on Grace, he realized she was a breath away from killing his V.P of Operations. For some infernal reason, Jackson and Grace had never gotten along. Which made what he was about to propose just this side of insane.

"Before you two disintegrate into another of your fascinating arguments, I have something to say."

Jackson narrowed his eyes. "To both of us?"

Merrick pulled Chloe to his side. Needing to feel her seemed as necessary as breathing. When she melted against him, peace stole through him. "Yeah, it concerns you both." His gaze rested on Grace. "I want Jackson to interview you for the position as marketing rep."

"Merrick, I don't—"

He cut Grace off with a hard look. "You said yourself you wanted to work for me. With your schooling, you're the most qualified person for the position."

"I figured you'd hire me to work for *you*. I didn't plan to be this dweeb's glorified gofer."

Merrick clenched his jaw as a headache started to come on. "You won't be a gofer. Jackson's solid. He'll show you the ropes and treat you right."

Grace stepped closer and planted her hands on her hips. "Maybe you've not been paying attention, but Jackson and I don't exactly see eye to eye."

"That's only because you're ten inches shorter than me, Gracie."

Jackson seemed to be having way too much fun with this. Merrick never could understand why the man seemed to take such pleasure in provoking Grace. "Christ, Jackson, can't you at least try to be nice?"

"Can I say something?"

He hadn't expected Chloe to want a say in it. Although, one of the things they'd learned since they'd started counseling was to respect each other's role in the business. At one time Vaughn's Business Solutions had been in his name alone. He'd fixed that error. Now the business was both of theirs, equally. It'd been another attempt to prove to Chloe that he was deadly serious about keeping her number one in his life.

Merrick nodded, encouraging her to go on. Chloe dove right in. "Grace, you won't get a better opportunity than this. You've worked hard to get that degree, and Merrick's offer is your reward. Besides, isn't this exactly what you wanted?"

Grace nodded and stayed silent, for once. Amazing.

As they walked away, Merrick quirked his lips and tugged his wife around to face him. "You're good."

Chloe laughed. "All I did was point out the obvious."

"What if they kill each other? This may end up a real bad idea."

"No, they won't. She's in love with him, and he's got the hots for her big time."

Merrick stiffened, every single one of his protective instincts kicking in. "The hell you say! He's way too damned old for her."

Chloe placed two fingers against his lips and said, "Shh, it's their business, not ours. And he's only thirty-two to her twenty-two. Not exactly a huge gap."

Merrick's gaze sought out the two antagonists, shocked to the core when he witnessed Jackson sliding his fingers through Grace's blonde hair. Grace stepped back, forcing Jackson to drop his hand. "He has no business thinking of her that way,"

Merrick muttered.

Chloe laughed, which had him as hard as a baseball bat. "Only because she's your little cousin and you're way too overprotective. Let it go. It'll all work out."

"I still don't like it," he grumbled.

Chloe smoothed her thumb over his bottom lip, adding extra fuel to the fire in his loins. He grabbed her wrist and sucked the digit into his mouth, then bit the fleshy tip. "Think of a way to escape, baby," he murmured around her finger. "I need you."

"I'll always need you, Merrick."

"Keep saying things like that and I'm hauling your ass out of here, regardless of the barbeque."

Suddenly, black smoke wafted around them, pulling them out of their lusty haze. Merrick turned toward the grill and groaned. The hamburgers resembled little charcoal discs. "I suck at cooking."

"It's okay, because you excel at *other* things."

Merrick ached to show her those other things, but his mother shouting from the patio door had him scowling instead. He looked up to see Lacey heading toward them with a fresh batch of hamburgers. Shit, it was going to be a long night.

The heated look in his sweet wife's eyes made him see the truth, though. As long as he had Chloe, he was ten feet tall and capable of anything.

Tempting Grace

Dedication

To Valerie, you see the things I don't and I'm so grateful for that! Thanks for being such a wonderful friend and for loving the Vaughn bunch as much as I do!

Prologue

Three years earlier

Grace looked in her rearview mirror and clutched the steering wheeler tighter. The eighteen-wheeler was coming on her too fast. Damn it. She should have taken her sister's advice and stayed at the dinner party until it stopped snowing or at least slowed down a bit. She hated driving on icy roads, especially at night. The snow made visibility extremely poor, and the truck behind her seemed intent on driving her right off the road. She could kick herself for offering to work tomorrow, Christmas Eve. She would be getting paid double-time, though, and she needed the extra cash for books. College, she was learning, wasn't cheap.

Still, when she'd left her sister's house, she hadn't expected to deal with a road-raging truck driver. He blew his horn again, and she wanted to scream. She was already in the slow lane. What more did the asshole want? Her anger got the better of her and she blew her horn. She breathed a sigh of relief when she noticed him merging into the other lane.

"Couldn't have done that seven miles back, though, could you, jerk?" she mumbled as he came up alongside her.

She noticed the big rig out of her peripheral vision. Suddenly he beeped his horn again, and Grace forced herself to keep her eyes on the road. This was going beyond normal road rage. She suddenly felt as if she'd been tossed into a bad horror movie. She reached over and turned up her radio, attempting to shut out her fears of being on the road alone with a psycho wielding a really big truck as a weapon. Just as the cheerful notes of a Christmas classic filled the interior of the car, the truck driver swerved. Time seemed to stand still as she watched the scene unfold around her. The fear of being crunched under tons of metal had her slamming her foot into the brake pedal. Her car spun out of control. The sounds of breaking glass and metal connecting with metal mingled with the cheerful notes of the song still coming from the speakers. The last thing she heard before the world went black was Bing singing about a white Christmas.

♦

"She should have waited. I told her to wait."

Grace heard the worry in her sister's voice and she wanted to reassure her, but she didn't quite understand what had her so upset to start with. It was almost like she was crying, but why?

"We know, Faith. She'll be okay."

Merrick? Why was Merrick in her dorm room? Come to think of it, why was her sister in her dorm room? And why the hell couldn't she seem to get her eyelids to open?

"I should have made her stay," Faith wailed. "This is all my fault. I insisted she come to the dinner party. She's been studying so hard, and I thought the break would do her good. This is my fault."

"No, it isn't, now stop that or I'll paddle your ass," Merrick growled. "This is because of a drunk truck driver. No one else is to blame."

"Merrick's right, dear. Grace is a strong girl, she'll be okay," her mother said, her voice as soothing as ever. "Though I could kick myself for letting her drive that old Nova. I should've insisted on a car with airbags."

Then Grace remembered. Oh, God, the truck, the icy roads. She remembered it all. Grace concentrated harder on opening her eyes. Finally the blurry outlines of her mother, sister and Merrick came into view. She blinked a few times and tried her voice. "Hey," she muttered, though it sounded like someone had scraped her throat with sandpaper. Crap, it hurt worse than the time she'd had Mono.

"She's coming around," her mother announced. "Someone get the doctor."

"Where am I?" Grace wheezed.

"It'll be okay, kiddo," her sister said, tears streaming down her cheeks. "You're in the hospital. There was a car accident."

Grace licked her lips and tried to move, but her entire body was one big ache. "There was a truck," she said to the room at large. "He wouldn't stay off my tail."

"We know," Merrick gritted out. "The asshole lived, but he's in critical condition. He tested two times the legal limit for alcohol. He was drunk as hell. I don't think he's going to be driving again anytime soon."

She wiggled her toes and was actually grateful they hurt. "My left leg feels like someone tried to massage it with a sledgehammer, and my stomach is on fire."

"You suffered a few broken bones, sweetie," her mother explained. "And there was some trauma to your abdomen, but you'll be okay now. Everything will be okay, you'll see. I love you."

"I had my seatbelt on," she said, as if anyone cared about that now.

"Of course you did," her mother said. "You're a smart girl, Grace, always have been."

The door opened and her dad stepped in, doctor in tow. Her dad looked as if he'd aged ten years. She tried to smile, to reassure him she was okay, but it hurt too much.

"You just lie still, baby," he said as he came to the side of the bed and took her hand. She relaxed instantly. Her dad could always take her pain away. When she was a kid, she used to think her dad was some kind of magician. She still wasn't so sure he wasn't.

She watched as the doctor checked her heart rate then began to palpitate her abdomen. She winced when he pushed on the area below the left side of ribs. He frowned and stepped back. "I want to run a few tests."

"What sort of tests?" her mother asked as she clutched onto her dad's hand. His arm came around her shoulders and he pulled her close. Faith stood on the other side, next to Merrick. Everyone in the room looked worried. Grace just wanted to go back to sleep. God, she was tired.

"They gave you some meds, that's why you're so groggy." Merrick answered her unspoken question.

"Must be some good stuff. I feel like I could sleep for a week."

'You've already been out for two days straight."

"No way." Merrick nodded, his expression serious. Grace sighed. "I totally screwed up Christmas, huh?"

Merrick chuckled. "We forgive you, brat."

Grace wanted to come back with something smart-alecky, but her voice wouldn't work. Her eyelids drifted closed, and suddenly she just didn't care about tests and crazy truck drivers. All she wanted to do was sleep.

♦

"Are you telling me I'll never be able to have kids? Isn't there some sort of surgery or something?"

The doctor shook his head, his face kind and gentle. "That's not what I'm saying at all. The tear in your uterus will just make you a higher risk for miscarriage. With proper care there's every possibility for you to have plenty of healthy children."

Grace slumped against the back of the bed. "No airbags. I shouldn't have insisted on that stupid car. At the time it seemed cooler than some dumb, four-door sedan."

"True the airbags would have prevented this type of injury, but the truth is that muscle car probably saved your life, Grace. Cars were built a lot more solid back in the seventies. That tank of a car you were driving protected you."

She was glad to hear that, at least, though she thought the doctor was probably just trying to make her feel like less of an idiot. She'd been in the hospital for a week while the doctors ran their tests and took way too many vials of blood and basically drove her up the freaking wall. She thought all the hoopla was just nonsense. She felt fine, other than some muscle ache and the annoying cast on her leg. Then again, she never expected to hear the news that the trauma she'd suffered to her abdomen would somehow be permanent. Bruises, nothing more. Those hopes were dashed now. The news left her numb. She hadn't really thought a lot about having kids, what nineteen-year-old college freshman did? Still she hadn't expected the good doc to tell her about a tear in her uterus.

Sometimes life had a way of really sucking.

Two Years Later

"You sure you won't play at least one more game? I'll be easy on you."

Blade laughed and swiped at the sweat on his brow. "That competitive streak is going to get you in a world of trouble one of these days, Jackson."

Grace watched her cousin and one of Merrick's employees play a game of HORSE. She'd never seen anyone smoke Blade in basketball before. She eyed the newcomer, noting the tall frame and muscular body clad in nothing but a pair of khaki shorts. He'd taken off his shirt and currently used it as a sweat rag. He looked delicious. She wouldn't mind being the sweat rag. Sliding over his chest and rock hard abs would be a delight.

"My competitive streak is nothing compared to yours. We both know I never would have gotten you to agree to three games if you hadn't wanted to beat me so much."

Blade guzzled his bottled water and swiped his hand over his mouth. "I figure someone needs to put you in your place. Might as well be me."

"Yeah, too bad it didn't work for you." Jackson dribbled the ball a few times before throwing it in the vicinity of the basket.

Grace concentrated was on the way Jackson sucked down his own bottle of water. Geez, even that normal act seemed sexy as hell. Then it hit her. Literally. She'd been balanced on the edge of the rail of the porch. The momentum behind the ball knocked her off her precarious perch, and she fell right on her ass. Had she been paying any attention to the ball, she would have noticed it coming straight at her.

"Shit," she mumbled.

Blade and Jackson both rushed to her side. Blade helped her up, concern on his face. "You okay, brat?"

She didn't want to look at Jackson. She already felt like the biggest fool. "Fine, just bruised my ego a bit, I think."

"Sorry about that," Jackson said. "I wasn't paying attention."

She made a point of brushing off her jean shorts. "No big. I've taken worse playing football with this slug." She pointed to Blade.

When she finally allowed herself to glance over at Jackson, she knew two things. One, he was way more of a hunk close up. Two, he was going to be really hard to ignore now that she'd gotten a good healthy look at him.

Jackson held out his hand. "Jackson Hill. I work for Merrick."

Grace took it and smiled. "I know who you are. I'm Grace Vaughn, the annoying younger cousin."

"And I'm out of here," Blade grumbled. "I need to find some air conditioning."

"You're getting old and soft. Better watch it, I think I see a pot belly in your future," she teased Blade, though it was the furthest thing from the truth. Blade was all muscle. She secretly thought fat cells were merely too afraid to venture anywhere near him.

"You like to play with fire, don't you, Gracie?"

Oh, hell, he had a really nice voice. Deep, mysterious, full of wicked promise. "It's Grace, and Blade's a big boy, he can handle some razzing."

"I agree," he murmured. He fell silent, staring at her as if imagining things. Naughty things. Grace had the urge to yank at the hem of her black tank top to cover her exposed abdomen. The tank and shorts had seemed like a good idea for a hot July family get together. The way Jackson licked his lips and kept glancing at her belly and legs made her wish she'd worn a sweatshirt and jeans.

"I've never seen you at one of the Vaughn picnics," she said in an attempt at normalcy. "Why is that?"

He sat on the edge of the porch and crossed his arms over his chest. "I wasn't invited until now. Merrick and I have gotten to be pretty good friends, though."

"Golf?"

He chuckled, which was oh-so-yummy. "Yeah. Merrick and I both love it."

"Male bonding, how cute," she said, hoping to shake his calm demeanor.

He looked over at the basketball sitting on the porch floor, bent and picked it up. "Do you like to play, Gracie?"

She refused to enjoy the way he said her name. No one called her Gracie. She'd always hated it. Jackson made it sound sinful. "I play some, yeah."

"Feel up to playing a game with me?"

The double-entendre wasn't lost on her or her libido. "Your timing is off. I was about to leave when you smacked me in the face with that thing."

He suddenly stood and cupped her chin. When he turned her head to the left and right, Grace was too stunned to move. Apparently satisfied, he smiled. "You're too pretty to be bruised."

"Thanks," she said. Escape. She had to escape. The man was lethal and way out of her league. She liked simple guys. Guys she could easily handle. Jackson was neither. She started around him. "It was nice meeting you," she tossed over her shoulder.

"Maybe one of these days you'll play with me, Gracie."

His words caught her, and she froze. It took all her strength to get her feet moving again. She didn't think she breathed until she sat behind the wheel. Grace looked down at her hands and they actually shook. "He's just a guy, quit acting like such a girl," she chastised herself.

It was a good five minutes before she could pull the keys out of her pocket and start the car. His words played over and over in her head.

Chapter One

Present day

"He's driving me insane. I can't work with him, Merrick. You have to do something."

"Calm down, Grace, and tell me what the problem is...this time."

Grace counted to ten and tried to concentrate on not losing her cool. It wasn't easy. "He's a Neanderthal," she stated. "I want to work for you. Not him."

"Tattle-telling again, Gracie?"

Every muscle in her body went rigid at that deep baritone. She turned around and had to brace herself when she saw Jackson lounging against the doorjamb to Merrick's office. "Don't you ever knock?"

He winked, which only infuriated her more. "The door wasn't closed, and your voice tends to carry. I was curious what had you all in a tizzy."

She stepped toward him and gritted out, "Call me Gracie one more time and I'll—"

"Enough!" Merrick shouted. "Both of you, get in here and close the damn door."

Grace recognized the tone. Merrick rarely got angry, but when he did it was wise not to push him. She stepped closer to his desk and sat in a chair facing him. She refused to look at Jackson, though she could hear the door close behind her.

"Sit down, Jackson," Merrick said, his voice brooking no argument. Out of the corner of her eye, Grace saw Jackson taking the chair next to her. "Grace, I asked you to work with Jackson because that's where you're needed right now. I need a marketing rep, and that's what you're good at. With Chloe five months into her pregnancy, I need Jackson to pick up some of my slack. That means you need to pick up some of his slack. You knew this when you took the job."

Grace drooped. It was all true. She had known what she was getting into. She'd wanted to work at her cousin's company so badly she'd purposely squashed her concerns about working alongside the much too attractive Jackson Hill. The man put her on edge, and she'd never understood why. He simply rubbed her the wrong way. Or maybe the real problem was that he rubbed her just exactly right, which scared her. She didn't like being scared. It pissed her off.

"I need to know if this is going to work," Merrick said, his gaze bouncing from her to Jackson then back again. "You two have been going at it for the full two months you've been here. It's driving me crazy, and I can't afford to be any crazier than I already am right now. The baby will be here soon and I need to focus."

"I don't see the problem," Jackson said, his voice full of confidence. "Grace is a good worker. I have no beef with her whatsoever."

She clasped her hands in her lap and just barely kept herself from saying something she'd regret. "The only problem I have is that you can't take no for an answer."

He chuckled. "Really? Because I don't recall asking a question."

Technically, it was true. He hadn't asked her on a date. But he'd hinted. At times it even seemed he took great pleasure in pushing her, making her imagine things she had no business imagining. Having sexual fantasies about her boss was surely a no-no. She peeked over at him and caught him staring at her. The heat in his gaze couldn't be missed. He wanted her. He might not have spelled it out, but the signals were there. She'd effectively evaded them too. Working every day with him was stealing her control, though. She'd snap soon, and then where would she be? Just another of Jackson Hill's conquests, she was sure of it. He hadn't tried to hide the fact that he wasn't into long term relationships. And she wasn't interested in being a notch on his belt. That left her with one solution. Quit working at Vaughn's Business Solutions. The thought made her gut clench.

"I want to talk to Jackson alone for a minute. Take a break, okay?"

She saw something in Merrick's expression that worried her. He'd had the same look the day Ronny Walsh had put a tack on her chair in her seventh grade science class. She'd made the mistake of crying about it in front of Merrick. She didn't know what Merrick did, but the next day Ronny had come to her with an apology. It hadn't been her intention to get Jackson in trouble, only convince Merrick to transfer her so she wasn't in such close proximity to the infernal man. She suddenly felt very guilty.

"I'm not sure that's a good idea," she said, unable to hide the worry in her voice.

Merrick looked down at his watch, then back at her. "It's noon, time for lunch anyway."

Merrick wasn't letting up. She would get nowhere with him now. Grace sighed and stood, but as she glanced over at

Jackson, she was surprised to notice he didn't seem at all concerned. Did the man have no sense of self-preservation? When he winked, she wanted to throttle him. She threw her hands in the air. "I give up. I'm going job hunting. I'll be back in an hour."

As she yanked the door open, she wondered for the hundredth time why she'd thought she could handle working with Jackson Hill. Surely she'd been under some sort of spell when she'd accepted Merrick's job offer. There simply wasn't any other explanation.

♦

It was all Jackson could do not to laugh as he watched Grace stalk out of Merrick's office. He'd gotten to her, and she was running scared. It was only a matter of time now. He'd been lusting after the little blonde imp from the moment he'd spotted her at one of Merrick's family's cookouts. He'd tried the subtle approach, but that had gotten him exactly nowhere. She'd shot him down like a clay pigeon. The more he'd gotten to know her, the more he'd come to realize that Grace used sarcasm to keep people at arm's length. Especially him. She was damned good at holding him off. Jackson was getting desperate. If he didn't get her to submit soon, he'd explode.

"Quit thinking about her."

Merrick's voice dragged him back to reality. "I wasn't," Jackson lied.

Merrick rolled his eyes and sat back in his chair. "What the hell is it with you two? I can't figure it. It's as if you like fighting with her."

"The truth?"

"No, I'd rather you lied to me," Merrick ground out. "Yes, I want the truth."

"Just remember, you asked," he warned. "Fighting with Grace is like foreplay. It turns us both on. She wants me as much as I want her. She just can't seem to let her guard down long enough to let me in. I've yet to figure out why." He leaned forward in the chair and said, "Maybe you can help me with that one."

Merrick shook his head. "You are aware that I'm not only her cousin, but your boss, right?"

Jackson recognized Merrick in overprotective mode. But Jackson had no intention of staying away from Grace, now or ever. "Is this the part where you warn me away?"

"Grace is my employee, and I protect my employees. You're in dangerous territory, flirting with her. Sexual harassment isn't something I take lightly, Jackson."

Jackson went rigid. "Did she say I sexually harassed her?"

"That's not the point. The point is I protect what's mine."

"I would never hurt Grace."

"But you *are* making her uncomfortable, and I can't have that. Either back off or I'll move her to a different position."

Merrick had just tossed down the gauntlet. If Jackson pushed the issue he could lose Grace and probably his job, not to mention his friendship with Merrick. Still, he wasn't about to make a promise he knew damn well he couldn't keep. Jackson rubbed his jaw and decided to lay it all on the line.

"This isn't a game to me. I care about your cousin. You can fire me, pull Grace under your wing or whatever, but I won't stop pursuing her until *she* tells me to stop."

Merrick slammed his fist on the desk. "What the hell is up with you? I've never seen you act like this. You've never dated an employee. Why Grace?"

Jackson had wondered that himself. "She's the most annoying woman I've ever met. She tells me to go to hell and I get a fucking hard-on. She threatens to maim me and I start drooling. Damned if I can figure it out. But until I do, I won't let up. She wants me, she's just fighting it. I scare her." Jackson rubbed his jaw and thought for a second. "No, that's not right. I think the idea of being with me scares her."

"Grace doesn't scare easily," Merrick mused. "But you're right. She's been watching you like a caged lioness. If you aren't careful, she'll have you for lunch. Grace can be damned mean when cornered."

It was now or never. Time to make a deal with the devil. "I have a solution. One that will please everyone."

Merrick drummed his fingers on the desk for several seconds before saying, "I'm listening."

"The Interop Convention in Vegas is coming up," Jackson stated, referring to the nation's biggest information technology convention. Businesses from all over the world attended to view new cutting-edge technologies. It was May, and the convention was a week away. "I want to take Grace with me when I go. If she's still resisting my irresistible charms after that, I'll back off."

"You and Grace in Las Vegas for a week? You think I'll agree to this?"

"I think you want Grace to be happy. I think you want harmony back in your office. Let me take Grace to Vegas. Not the whole week. Three days, that's all I'm asking, and I promise you'll have both."

Merrick got out of the chair and paced. Jackson was almost afraid he was going to fire his ass right then. He had every right too. Jackson was surprised when Merrick said, "If Grace wants to go, I won't stop her. But it's her choice, not yours. You won't force her because you're her boss. Understood?"

Jackson said a silent prayer that Grace wouldn't fight him on this one. "Understood."

Merrick came around the desk and leaned against the edge. "One more thing."

Jackson stood, sensing a battle coming. "Yeah?"

"Grace is like a sister to me, to Blade and Lacey too. I'd be very careful with her if I were you."

He nodded. "I know how close you all are, but this is between Grace and me."

Merrick crossed his arms over his chest. "Grace is all grown up now. Chloe says she can take care of herself, but that doesn't mean I won't kick your ass if you make her cry. Remember that while you're trying to sweet talk her into going to Sin City with you."

Jackson laughed. "Hold off on buying the tar and feathers until after I get back, will ya? I wouldn't want you to waste your money."

Merrick shook his head. "You have to get her to agree to the trip first. I'm not so convinced you've got what it takes."

"We'll see."

"Yeah, we will."

Merrick called his name as Jackson started to leave. He stopped as he reached the door and turned. "Yeah?"

"Has Grace told you about her car accident?"

Jackson's stomach bottomed out. "What car accident?"

"When she was nineteen, she was in a real bad wreck. We weren't sure she was going to make it those first twenty-four hours. It was hard on all of us. The thing is, Grace is the youngest of the Vaughns. I guess you could say she's sort of the baby we'd all like to wrap in cotton if she'd only let us." Merrick paused before adding, "If you really care about her, you should know the accident left a lasting impression on Grace."

Jackson squeezed the doorknob. "In what way? Emotionally?"

"Ask her that."

He nodded and opened the door. As he made his way down the hall to his own office, an image of a beat-up nineteen-year-old Gracie sprang to mind, and it nearly made Jackson throw up. He didn't like thinking of her as fragile. She was usually so tough and she handled herself so well around him it was easy to forget just how delicate she really was.

Chapter Two

Grace sauntered back into the office, feeling better than she had in weeks. She'd taken a two hour lunch. The first hour had been spent sucking down a latté and devouring a grilled chicken Caesar salad while she attempted to make future lunch plans with some of her old business contacts. She wasn't convinced it would get her anywhere as far as a job offer, but it never hurt to try. The second hour she'd taken the time to go to her cousin Lacey's gym and get in a workout. It didn't quite take away all her frustrations, but it had helped.

Now as Grace moved through the office and spotted Candice, they both smiled a greeting. It still surprised Grace that Candice and Blade were married, much less soon-to-be parents of a baby boy. The marital bliss and pregnancies in the Vaughn family were enough to make a single woman envious.

As she approached her desk, Grace wrapped the strap of her purse around the back of the chair and sat. She tried to concentrate on the new software she'd been working on, but it wasn't any use. All she saw was Jackson's grin as she'd walked out of Merrick's office. It'd been juvenile of her to take her problems to her cousin. She should have known the way Merrick would react. He was always much too protective of her. She could go into Jackson's office and confront him, make him tell her what the two men had said after she'd left. Had Merrick fired him, punched him, or both?

"Stop frowning; your face will stick that way one of these days."

Grace looked up from the flat screen monitor to find Jackson grinning down at her, his hands in his pockets. God, the man was yummy. His close-cropped dark hair and chiseled cheekbones had always made her think of a tough guy from an action movie. His hard, muscular frame wasn't anything to overlook either. For the first time she wondered if he'd ever been in the military. He seemed ex-something. SEAL. Marine. Sniper. Dangerous and sexy, both of those words described Jackson Hill's powerful physique and hypnotic silver eyes.

"So, no black eye. Am I to assume you two didn't engage in a fist fight then?"

He tsked. "We're adults. We solve things like men, not prickly teenagers."

She let that one pass, though she had at least a dozen good comebacks on the tip of her tongue. "Still have a job?"

Jackson pulled his hands out of his pockets and braced himself against her desk. As he leaned down, she could smell his masculine scent, like the jungle, wild and untamed. "Hoping Merrick fired me?"

Her cheeks burned at his words. "I shouldn't have gone to Merrick. I'm sorry."

Jackson reached out and touched her cheek. "That almost seemed sincere, Gracie."

She jerked backward, out of his reach, and growled, "Screw it, I'm not sorry."

Jackson's grin disappeared. "Come into my office. I need to talk to you."

"Jackson, this isn't—"

He cut her off with a hand in the air. "I need a little privacy. Please?"

Grace didn't really have a choice at that point and she damn well knew it. Jackson was simply too adorable when he murmured please in that sexy baritone of his. She stood, but before she could follow him into his office, she asked, "Were you ever in the military?"

His head cocked to the side. "Yeah, the Marines. I did a four-year enlistment right out of high school. Why?"

She sighed. "Just curious."

"Uh, okay." He turned and started toward his office, Grace watched the way his ass moved beneath his black dress slacks. God, the man was delicious. A squeeze. Just one squeeze and she could live the rest of her life with a grin on her face.

As he closed the door to his office, panic welled up. Most men didn't send her blood rushing through her veins, and she never felt panicky around them. With Jackson she was the helpless field mouse cornered by the hungry tom cat. Not a happy image.

Jackson moved around his desk and sat, indicating she should sit in one of the chairs across from him. She sat and braced herself, unsure what this new mood of his was all about. He seemed pensive, and she wasn't used to that. Jackson was usually flirtatious or ribbing her until she wanted to pull out her hair, or his. Those were moods she could handle. This serious side had her fidgeting in her seat.

"I want to know why you went to Merrick. Is it so horrible working for me?"

Grace clutched the arm of the chair. He was asking for the truth. Since the moment she'd started at Merrick's company, Jackson had never actually pushed her into dealing with their mutual attraction. He seemed content to let them dance around each other. Dodging him and suppressing her insane attraction to him had just become a thing of the past, though.

"It's not so bad. You pissed me off and I reacted. I'm sorry."

He glanced down at his desk and frowned, then moved a few files around. As he leaned back and crossed his arms over his chest, he said, "Yeah, that's the part I'm fuzzy on, Gracie. What set you off? One minute I was talking to you like any other co-worker, just shooting the breeze, the next thing I know you're growling and stomping off. What did I say?"

She would have to admit it now, or try to lie. She sucked at lying to Jackson. He always saw right through her, somehow. Another infuriating thing about the man. "You were talking about your night with Ginger," she blurted.

"Ginger? What does she have to do with anything?"

She rolled her eyes and stood. "You know, for an educated man, you can be so dense." Grace started for the door, but she never managed more than a few feet before a pair of large, strong hands pulled her to a stop. She swung around and glared. "Let me go."

"You were jealous," he stated, as if she hadn't already figured out that part on her own.

"Hallelujah! Give the man a cigar."

"How do you think I felt when you threw Antonio in my face? And don't say you didn't mention him just to piss me off, because we both know the truth."

She'd gone out with Antonio, a cute guy from accounting, on the off chance she'd be able to forget about Jackson. It hadn't worked. She'd spent the entire evening comparing the two men, and she'd found Antonio lacking big time.

"I wasn't talking about Antonio like he was an all-you-can-eat buffet, though."

She watched a muscle in Jackson's jaw twitch angrily. It made her want to lean in and lick him. "Don't piss me off by lying. I respect the women I date. I don't expound on their *attributes* with friends and co-workers, and you know it. I mentioned going to dinner with her, that's all. You damn near shot out of my office like a cat that'd just gotten her tail stepped on."

His imagery stung her pride. "That's not true."

He leaned close and murmured, "Stop lying, sweetheart. You were jealous, same as I was when you mentioned Antonio."

She tugged her arm and got exactly nowhere. "Fine, I was jealous," she admitted. "Can I go now?"

"No. We need to fix this. We can't continue working together if you're going to run to Merrick every time you feel cornered."

She made a point of wiggling her arm. "Then stop cornering me."

He released her, and she stepped back. He stepped forward. Grace held her ground, though his nearness sent fire dancing through her veins and her pussy throbbed with need.

"You like it when I corner you," he said as he looked her over. "You're just too chicken to admit it."

Grace narrowed her eyes. "Take that back."

He grinned. "Nope. It's true. You're too chicken to take what you want, and we both know it."

"We work together. Getting involved is a bad idea." Crap, even she knew that was a lame excuse.

He pointed to the door. "Exhibit A: Chloe and Merrick."

Damn, she hated when he was right. "That's different. Merrick wasn't a stalker."

He laughed. "And I am?"

"You may as well be."

"How about you just prove you aren't a chicken. Put me in my place, Gracie."

She knew exactly where this was leading. "I suppose if I go out with you, it'll be proof. That's so pathetic."

He shook his head, looking entirely too sure of himself. "Go to the Interop Convention with me. Spend three days in Las Vegas by my side. Prove you can resist this chemistry arcing back and forth, and I'll leave you alone."

"You just want to get me drunk so you can take advantage of me. Perv."

Jackson stepped closer and touched the tip of her nose. It was completely platonic, nothing flirtatious in the touch at all, and yet he might as well have touched her breast, she was so turned on. "You know better than that. I would want you alert for what I have in mind." He paused before adding, "What do you say? Can you handle three days in Vegas with me? Or is it too much temptation for you?"

She should have walked out. *Turn around and walk away, don't let him suck you in.* The inner voice was ignored. Instead, she stepped forward, barely grazing his hard body with the tips of her breasts. Even through the material of their shirts, Grace felt her nipples harden as if begging for more. Jackson tensed. His gaze narrowed. The atmosphere around them seemed to fairly spark.

Grace lifted on her toes and whispered, "Bring it on."

Jackson licked his lips and cupped her chin in his palm. "You're going to push me too far one of these days, little girl."

Grace didn't speak. She couldn't if she'd wanted to. She just stood there, their bodies barely touching, Jackson staring at her gaping mouth. When he released her and stepped back, she nearly wilted. Had she wanted him to kiss her? Duh! Even

141

the thought sent her temperature higher.

Three days. Three whole days of Jackson Hill in Sin City. Yep, it was official. She'd lost her mind.

♦

Jackson watched Grace's quiet exit, her cute ass capturing his attention. The black slacks she wore fit just right, displaying her ass like the work of art it was. He didn't let himself smile until she'd pulled the door closed. He mentally started rearranging meetings. The convention was next week, and he had plenty to deal with between now and then. Thankfully he'd planned ahead and asked Candice to register him and Grace for the convention weeks ago. Candice had reserved two rooms and she'd also taken care of the flight details. The itinerary for the event sat on his desk for all to see. He'd been worried there for a minute, thinking Grace had spotted it. He'd covered it just in time.

Three days of Grace Vaughn. With any luck at all, they'd spend the entire time in bed, screw the convention. He imagined her naked, that sassy mouth wrapped around his cock as he licked her juicy pussy. Then Merrick's words sprang to mind, and once more he saw a broken and bleeding Grace, barely clinging to life.

Why hadn't she ever told him about it? Dumb question. They'd both been too busy verbally sparring, and Grace was particularly adept at keeping him at a distance. She guarded her emotions around him. He'd never been able to breech her defenses. A few times he'd come close, though. Once, when they'd gone to lunch together after Grace had lost a bet, he'd nearly gotten a kiss from her. He'd taken her to a Chinese restaurant and he'd actually managed to get her to relax, even

142

laugh. She'd been a breath away from kissing him that day. He'd been so shocked she'd let her guard down, he'd ended up blowing it. She hadn't let him take her to lunch again.

He'd been drawn to Grace since the day he'd accidently hit her in the face with a basketball. Her spunky attitude and quick wit had sucked him in. Each time they came into contact, she pushed him to the very limits of control without even trying. She could pull emotions out of him he hadn't known he possessed. One minute she'd have him laughing over her particular brand of sarcasm, the next he was ready to take her to bed. Jackson couldn't help but wonder if it was his age that caused her to hold back. Did the gap bother her? He couldn't be sure, but he knew one thing for certain, Grace wasn't at all superficial. There were depths to the woman that he desperately wanted to explore. He had a feeling it'd take a lifetime to learn all of her secrets.

While some women filled their lives with meaningless bullshit like manicured fingernails and expensive clothes, Grace concerned herself with work and family. She had an understated beauty and a straightforward attitude that he admired. She wore very little make-up and simple clothes. From what he could tell, she rarely dated, which pleased the hell out of him. When she'd gone out with Antonio, Jackson had wanted to pound the little weasel for encroaching on his territory, but reality had set in and he'd known the truth. He had no right to Grace. She could date whomever she wanted. He only hoped that soon that person would be him.

Chapter Three

Grace read the same sentence three times before she finally gave up and put the book down. Her heart just wasn't in it. The only thing on her mind was how much trouble her big mouth had gotten her into this time. Las Vegas. Three days alone with Jackson. Could she be any denser? What had possessed her to agree? He'd challenged her, and she never could resist a challenge. He'd known exactly what she'd do when he'd called her chicken.

After she'd agreed to go to the convention, she'd gone back to her desk and finished out her day thinking of ways to wiggle out of the agreement. She'd come up with zero ideas, mostly because to back out would prove she couldn't handle being alone with Jackson. He'd win. She was much too competitive to lose. That left her staring at her muted television at seven o'clock at night, when she should be enjoying her new haul of romance novels. She picked up the book she'd been dying to read and tried to push Jackson out of her head. She managed three pages before her doorbell rang. "A distraction, thank God."

Grace stepped over the black heels she'd kicked off earlier, then rose on her toes to peek through the eyehole on her apartment door. *Jackson?* She flung the door wide and said, "What are you doing here?"

His lips quirked. "Nice to see you too, Gracie."

"How did you know where I lived?" Grace made a point of not checking out his hot body, even though she desperately wanted to. If she looked at the black t-shirt that was sure to be stretched across a muscular chest and tight jeans cupping his package, she'd start stuttering or something.

He propped his hand on her doorjamb. "Uh, I'm your boss, remember?"

"Right, dumb question."

"I don't suppose you're going to let me in," he said as his gaze took in the living room behind her.

She sighed and stepped back. "Come in."

"Thanks." Jackson moved around her, their bodies touching as he passed. Every nerve ending went to code red status, as if to say *Yippee! About damn time we got him alone.*

"Nice digs you have here."

Grace had taken great care in decorating her apartment, and it did her heart good to have Jackson's genuine approval. She'd gone with an Oriental flare. Sleek, modern lines and smooth surfaces. She liked the fresh, clean feel.

"Very Zen-like."

Grace looked around and realized he was right. The furniture had been expensive, but worth it.

Jackson walked over to her bookcase and picked out a paperback. "I like the bookcase. I don't think I've ever seen a round bookcase before. Cool."

He was looking at her romance books. She really hoped it wasn't an erotic romance. "It's teak. It was pricey, but I liked the design." *Please, please don't be an erotic romance.*

"How did you manage an entire living room suite on your pay?"

145

Her cheeks heated. "I'm sort of still paying it off. Credit card."

"Ah," he said as he sat on her hand-carved love seat.

"So, would you like something to drink?"

"Got a beer?"

"Yeah, but it's light beer. Will that work?"

"Yep," he said, then flipped the book open and started reading as if he'd been doing it for years. He looked entirely too at home in her apartment. Her gaze shot to his crotch and...damn. She shouldn't have looked. She'd be drooling soon. Grace stalked out of the room. The sooner he drank his beer, the sooner he'd leave. She could get back to sulking in peace.

As she entered the kitchen, a horrible thought struck her. He was looking at her things. Touching her shelves. Probably reading something very steamy while she piddled around. The man was too curious for his own good. What had she been thinking when she let him in? She should have slammed the door in his face. She'd been too stunned, knocked off her guard. Jackson was entirely too adept at surprise attacks.

Then again, he'd sought her out. This went beyond text messaging or corralling her in the break room. Jackson was ten years older than her and most likely way more experienced with the opposite sex. What did he see in her? As she grabbed two beers from the refrigerator she thought of what all that experience could mean for her if she did choose to sleep with him. She'd wanted to. Imagined it. It was obvious he wanted her just as much. Somehow she knew that if she ever let her guard down enough to sleep with Jackson, she'd quite possibly fall for the infernal man. She didn't want to fall in love with him. She didn't want to fall in love with any man, for that matter. Even though she knew she still had a lot to offer a man, the possibility that she may never be able to carry a baby to full-term left her feeling inadequate.

As Grace brought their ice cold beer into the living room, she stopped abruptly when she saw Jackson sitting on her couch, legs spread in front of him, reading. God, the man was hot. His long, muscular legs and flat abs made her wish she was bold enough to crawl up his body and plant one on him. As she moved closer and read the title of the book, her face burned with embarrassment. Jackson seemed to sense her arrival and looked at her over the top of the paperback.

He waved the book in the air and said, "Interesting reading material you have here, baby."

Grace handed him a beer. He took it, and she gave in to the need to suck down several swallows before she sat in the chair adjacent to him. She held out her hand. "Give it to me."

"Funny, that's sort of what Libby said to Hunter. The exact phrase is, 'Please, take me, Hunter.'" Jackson read, trying and failing to sound girly. "'I need to feel you inside of me, my love.'"

"It's a very romantic adventure." Why did she care what he thought of her reading material? It was none of his business.

He grinned and waved the book back and forth. "It's smut. Good smut, but smut all the same."

"*Hunter's Pleasure* is not smut. It's a beautiful tale of love. A romantic take on historic battles and lost treasures. The struggle the hero and heroine face is an emotional rollercoaster ride. The author won an award."

"Oh, really?"

"Yes."

"Then why are you so embarrassed?"

"Laugh all you want, but I notice it's grabbed your attention."

Jackson glanced up, his eyes hot with unmistakable

arousal. "Have you read the part where Hunter rips Libby's gown off and takes her against a tree?"

Grace licked her lips and willed her voice to sound steady and calm. "It's my book, of course I read it."

Jackson stood, and Grace instinctively sank back into the chair. He wouldn't let her retreat. Suddenly he was bent over her, cupping her chin in his palm. "I think I'd like to take you against a tree. Under the moonlight, in the same rough, untamed way Hunter takes Libby."

"That's bound to get us arrested."

Without warning, he kissed her. His soft lips lingered a few seconds, drawing a moan from her, before he lifted and whispered, "Hmm, it'd be worth a night in jail."

The doorbell rang. Saved! She sped to the door and slung it open, so glad for the reprieve she didn't bother checking the peephole.

"Oh, my God! Jordan!" She flung herself into the man's arms. He laughed and wrapped himself around her, holding her tightly.

"What the hell?"

Grace winced and pulled out of Jordan's embrace. As she turned back around she noticed Jackson standing with his fists clenched at his sides. He was not a happy camper. Well, too bad. She could hug whomever she wanted. Grabbing Jordan by the hand, Grace pulled him inside her apartment and shut the door. "Jackson, this is my neighbor and very dear friend, Jordan Davies."

Jackson moved up beside her, close. As if to show the other man she was taken? She wasn't pleased by that notion and tried to discreetly step away, but he only followed her. Before they managed to turn it into a dance, Grace kept still and opted to get him back later for his arrogance.

"It's nice to meet you, Jordan," he said as he held out his hand. Jordan took it with a smile. "I was just making plans with Grace. She's coming to Vegas with me for a few days."

Okay, maybe she wouldn't wait until later.

Jordan raised an eyebrow. "Damn, Grace, I didn't even know you were dating anyone. You could have said something."

"I'm not dating him. It's a business thing, not pleasure."

"We'll see," Jackson replied a good dose of humor lacing his words.

Grace elbowed him in the ribs, but the imbecile never even flinched. "Do you have to be so impossible?"

His knowing grin had the palm of her hand itching to smack him. "He called me a chicken," she explained to Jordan.

Jordan crossed his arms over his chest and said, "And going to Vegas is going to prove you're not?"

"It's complicated," she growled.

"Not really," Jackson inserted. "In fact, I think it's pretty simple."

She stared daggers at him. Why couldn't she have magical powers or something? She could zap him into a toad or something. Refusing to engage in yet more verbal warfare, she attempted to put the focus on Jordan instead. "So, out with it. How long before you're deployed again?"

"I'll be stateside for the next six months, then I'm back in Iraq."

"Jordan is a hero," Grace told Jackson.

Jordan flashed a sexy smile. "At least that's what I tell the ladies."

It was odd she'd never been attracted to Jordan. He really was handsome with his sandy-blond hair and dimples. And he had dreamy brown eyes. They were so dark you could barely

149

make out the pupils. But in the two years she'd known him, Grace had never felt even the slightest bit turned-on by his flirtations. Jackson, on the other hand, had only to look at her to get her motor humming. Which was frustrating as hell, because she had the feeling Jordan would be way easier to handle.

She gave up thinking and headed for the kitchen, calling over her shoulder, "Your usual, Jordan?"

"Sounds great, hon," he answered in his normal laid-back way.

"Do you want another, Jackson?" Grace asked as she opened the refrigerator and grabbed a cold beer for her neighbor.

"No, thanks."

It wasn't the words, but the tone that had her biting her lip. Jackson sounded angry. In all the time she'd spent with him, she'd never heard that tone from him before. What had set it off?

She popped the top off the beer and went back into the room. Jordan was on her couch, legs spread, smiling at her. Jackson still stood, arms crossed over his massive chest and staring at Jordan as if he'd like to take him apart. One painful inch at a time.

She handed Jordan his drink, and he winked at her. She peeked at Jackson and saw his eyes narrow. He was jealous. Oh, now this could be fun. He deserved a little payback for his earlier comments about her romance books.

Grace went straight to the couch and sat next to Jordan. Not touching, but close enough. "I'm so glad you're back. I worry when you're away." Which was nothing but the truth. Being a U.S. Marine in this day and age wasn't anything to play around with.

The hand that wasn't holding the beer patted her thigh. "It's cool. I know to keep my head down."

Jackson came forward and sat on the other side of her, then slung an arm over her shoulders. Grace held back a grin and continued talking to Jordan.

"Of course you do. You're a very skilled man," she said.

Jordan cocked his head to the side and studied her a minute, then said, "Are you okay?"

"Of course, why wouldn't I be?"

Jordan shrugged and took a drink of his beer. "You look flushed, that's all."

Grace wanted to hide her head in the sand. Flushed, hell, she was damn near on fire with Jackson so close. She could smell that scent of his, and it drove her libido crazy. "I'm fine. I'm more interested in hearing about you."

"I'm thinking of asking Lisa to marry me. Think she'll say yes?"

Jordan and Lisa had been dating for two years, but the military life had taken its toll on their relationship. "I think she'd be crazy not to marry you."

Jordan leaned forward and murmured, "I would ask you, but you'd probably just drop-kick me."

She laughed, knowing he was full of it. "No, Lisa would drop-kick you."

He gave a mock shudder. "You're probably right. Lisa has a mean temper when she's riled."

"Oh, please, she's as sweet as a lamb."

He rolled his eyes. "You and Lisa both scare me."

She reared back. "Me?"

"I've seen your temper, Grace. You're not to be fooled with

when you're pissed."

She smacked his chest. "Oh, yeah, I'm so scary to a big, strong Marine like yourself."

Jordan laughed. "Good to see you're still as mouthy as ever, hun."

He took one last swig of his beer and set it on the coffee table, then stood. "Thanks for the beer." He leaned down, presumably to peck her on the cheek, but Jackson was quicker.

"Don't even think about it, Davies," Jackson growled, his voice a cold bite of steel. "And you can quit with the hun shit too. She's not your *hun.*"

"Damn it, Jackson," she scolded. "Jordan is from the south. To him everyone is hun or darlin'. It's like saying hello. He means nothing by it."

Jordan, being the goof, held out his hand and in a too-chipper voice teased, "It's been a very pleasant visit, Grace. Hope we can do this again sometime."

She wanted to throttle them both. And just to get under Jackson's skin, she ignored Jordan's hand, rose to her feet and quickly kissed his cheek.

"Grace," Jackson warned. He stood and towered over them both. "Paybacks are hell, baby."

And why that gave her a delicious shiver, Grace had no clue.

Chapter Four

Jackson stared at Grace as she closed and locked the apartment door. They were alone again, just the way he liked it. But first he had to know the truth. "You did that on purpose," he stated. "You like to tease."

She pointed at him. "You were being all territorial. I don't belong to you, Jackson, so stop acting like I do."

He moved toward her, watching closely as she stepped around him. She did that a lot whenever he was near. Always put distance between them. "Maybe not, but you can't say my kiss didn't affect you."

She grabbed the empty bottles of beer and went to the kitchen. He followed her, as she no doubt knew he would. When she turned toward him, he saw a vulnerability he hadn't noticed before. Jackson was suddenly reminded of her age. She was twenty-two. He shouldn't even be in her apartment, much less planning a decadent three days in Vegas with her. While his mind knew the right thing to do, his body didn't really care.

"So it affected me," she finally admitted. "That doesn't mean you get to act the jealous lover around my friends."

"I'm in unfamiliar territory here, baby. I'm not your lover, not your friend. What the hell am I?"

"My boss."

He dragged his fingers through his hair and counted to ten. "I'm more than your boss, admit that much at least."

Grace bit her lip and stared at the floor. "You're more than my boss."

Jackson felt like shouting. It was a very tiny step, but at least he was getting somewhere. "Do you want me?"

She made an irritated sound. "You just don't give up, do you?"

He moved closer until their bodies were separated by only a few feet of linoleum. "Hell, I probably have no business being here. I'm way too damned old for you. And your entire family would skin me alive if they knew what I was thinking right now. But I'm not giving up. Not until you tell me straight out that you aren't attracted to me. If you can say that with total honesty, then I'll leave you alone. I won't bother you again. You have my word." *I only pray I can keep it.*

"I don't want you to leave me alone," she whispered. It was so faint he barely heard her. He started forward, but she shook her head. "But I need time. I'm not ready."

Jackson forced himself to stay still, to keep from spooking her. For whatever reason, Grace was afraid of being intimate with him. A crazy thought struck. "Are you a virgin?"

Her cheeks turned pink. "No! Geez, Jackson!"

He grinned. "A guy likes to know these things ahead of time."

"Can we please change the subject now?"

He thought of the reason he'd shown up at her apartment to begin with and said, "Actually I came here to ask you something."

"What?"

"I wanted to know about your accident."

Grace stood straighter and placed one hand on her hip. "Merrick told you, didn't he?" He let his silence speak for him. "I'm going to kill him."

"Kill him later. Right now I want to know what happened. Will you tell me?"

"I suppose if I don't you'll just ask Merrick."

He shrugged, neither confirming nor denying.

She sighed. "Fine. Let's go back out to the living room."

Grace sat in the chair again, which irritated the shit out of him. He wanted her closer. "Afraid I have cooties or something?"

"More like I'm afraid you'll try to molest me."

Jackson made a cross over his heart. "I promise to be a good boy. Come on, Gracie, sit next to me."

No one was more surprised than he when she stood and sat on the couch. Their bodies weren't touching, but it was progress. If he moved an inch he'd be able to feel her curves.

He really wanted to move an inch.

"Touch me and you'll be icing your crotch for a week."

The woman was psychic. And scary. "You warned me," he pointed out. "I must be growing on you."

She laughed, and Jackson felt triumphant. She rarely laughed. Snarled, cursed under her breath, but rarely laughed around him. A man could grow to enjoy Gracie's laughter. "So, tell me about the wreck. Merrick said it was pretty bad."

"It was the day before Christmas Eve. I was driving home from my sister's house. She'd been having a dinner party for some friends. It had snowed a lot that day. The roads were a mess. I should have stayed at my sister's place, but I'd promised to work the next day."

Since the day they'd met, he knew one truth, Grace was nothing if not loyal to her word. "Where'd you work?"

155

"At a grocery store. I needed the money for textbooks. I was a freshman in college at the time." She paused. "I thought the truck driver was just being annoying. I didn't know he'd been drinking. He swerved, I braked. Next thing I know I'm waking up in the hospital with broken bones and a headache."

"Damn."

She nodded. "Yeah. I was out for two days. Totally missed Christmas."

He sensed she was glossing over the worst of it. "What else, Grace?"

When she turned her head and their gazes met. "What do you mean?"

He put his arm around the back of the couch, careful not to touch her. "You're not telling me everything. What else happened?"

"It's not a big deal."

"Then tell me," he prompted. He wouldn't let her hide from him, though she seemed to be really good at doing exactly that most days.

She smoothed a hand over her forehead and said, "Fine. The steering wheel pushed into my abdomen. The trauma caused some damage to my uterus. It's not that I can't have kids, but I'm high risk for miscarriages."

He suddenly pictured Grace pregnant. She'd be beautiful. A woman like her would want kids, he thought. He could already picture her teaching a little blonde haired imp how to play chess and basketball and all the other games Grace excelled at. He thought of what she'd said about the steering wheel and frowned. "No air bags?"

"The car was old, it didn't come equipped."

He cupped her chin and stroked her jaw. "I'm sorry,

sweetheart."

She sat up straighter and moved away, forcing him to drop his hand. "I'm lucky to be alive."

"But it bothers you, doesn't it? You want kids."

"Yeah, it bothers me. I would've liked being a mom."

"You still can though, right? The option wasn't taken from you completely."

She nodded and started picking at some invisible spot on her black slacks. "The option is there, but with the scare of miscarriage hanging over my head," she shrugged, "I don't know. It seems like the odds are stacked against me."

"With a good doctor, the right attitude and a little faith, a lot can happen."

She smiled, and it warmed his heart. "Thanks for saying that."

He winked and wrapped his arm around her shoulders, pulling her closer. "You're too stubborn to let percentages keep you from having what you want. Even I know that much."

"Thanks...I think," she said.

He leaned toward her, noting the way her lips parted and her breathing increased. "You know what I think, Gracie?"

"W-What?"

"I think if I don't kiss you, I'll die," he murmured as he closed the gap between them and pressed his lips to hers. Jackson inhaled her gasp of surprise and pulled her close. As his tongue dipped inside her mouth, Jackson knew he'd been right about one thing: Grace's kiss was definitely potent.

Grace couldn't think, couldn't move. Jackson pressed his lips to hers. His tongue played and teased. Her body turned to liquid fire in two seconds flat. She should push him away, send him home. Instead, she lifted her arms and wrapped them around his neck. Jackson groaned as if pleased with her response, slid his arm beneath her knees and pulled her into his lap. Her body seemed so light against so much power and strength. It devastated her senses.

He lifted his mouth from hers and whispered something against her skin, then moved his lips downward, teasing her beyond measure. Grace leaned back, giving him permission to lick a fiery path along her chin and collarbone, before he zeroed in on the V of her ivory colored blouse. He kissed her cleavage and dipped his talented tongue beneath her white satin bra. She arched against him, desperate for more, so hungry for his touch all over.

Jackson chuckled and stopped long enough to murmur, "Easy, Gracie. We'll get there, I promise."

She didn't like that answer to her body's demands. "Faster or you can leave, damn it."

Jackson stopped his ministrations and stared at her in the brightly lit room. What went through his head in that moment was anyone's guess. When he touched her cheek, she practically melted at the tender caress.

"Is that what you really want, baby? Do you want me to leave?"

She hadn't expected him to take her seriously. She'd only been trying to get him moving along, to quit dawdling.

"No. I'm just..."

"Anxious?" he helpfully supplied.

She clenched her eyelids shut and admitted, "Yes."

Jackson's lips against her forehead forced her to open her eyes once more. His gaze held a wealth of tenderness. Butterflies came to life inside her. An entire swarm of them fluttered around in there.

"I like you like this. Anxious, wanting me. I've wanted you for months, but you were so damn good at evading me." He paused as if carefully choosing his next words. "Rushing isn't an option, baby. I like to take my time with a woman. A good, long time."

"You talk too much, Jackson. That's always been your downfall. All talk, no action."

"You're mean when you're horny." He grinned and let his gaze travel over her torso. "Fuck, you're a vision. I think I'd like to keep you for my pet."

She smacked him on the chest. "That's the most sexist thing I've ever—"

He effectively cut her off with a press of his lips to the pulse in her neck.

"Oh, my God," Grace moaned as she dug her fingers into his closely cropped dark hair, holding him firmly while he suckled her skin. She ached to feel those lips and that tongue lower. Much lower.

As if she'd spoken the thought aloud, Jackson inched downward, touching off several spasms as he went. Air brushed against her stomach, and she realized he'd somehow managed to unbutton her blouse and pull it down her shoulders, exposing her torso. When his tongue flicked over one hard nipple through the soft material of her bra, Grace nearly shot off the couch. She forgot her misgivings. Her body craved his touch. It'd been so long since she'd had sex. So damn long since she'd derived any real pleasure from a man's body.

As if afraid she would break, Jackson lightly ran his tongue back and forth over her areola seconds before sucking her nipple into his warm mouth, satin and all. He hummed in satisfaction, and the raspy vibration of his voice tormented her. Somehow Grace found herself sprawled, Jackson's hands on either side of her body effectively pinning her to the cushions. He surrounded her. His lethal strength and intoxicating scent filled her vision and her senses.

While he switched to the other breast, Grace marveled at his patience. He sipped at her skin and toyed with erogenous zones she wasn't aware she possessed. When he appeared to be settling in for a damned meal, Grace urged him lower with a tug on his hair. He obliged and moved his loving torture south. Her body reacted with a flow of moisture to her center. Every inch of her was ready for him to take her. To fuck her. He'd be hard and savage, she knew it in her bones.

"Please, Jackson."

A grunt was the only indication he'd even heard her plea. By tiny increments, he tugged her slacks down, and with each piece of flesh he exposed he sprinkled her with kisses. By the time the material was all the way off, Grace's pussy throbbed.

He sat back on his haunches, his gaze devouring her. "You don't wear panties?"

Grace didn't like embarrassment, and at that moment, she seemed to be swimming in it. "Wow, pretty observant. No wonder you're the VP."

"All night you sat here chatting with Jordan and you weren't wearing panties." He passed a hand over his face and grumbled, "Damn, Grace. You sure know how to drive a man crazy."

"Oh, gee, such a sweet talker you are."

He reached down and cupped her mound. "You're a real smart ass. One of these days I'm going to spank you for it too."

"Spanking my ass. Sounds kinky."

"Who said anything about your ass?" he growled. "I think I'd rather tie up these pretty tits and spank those instead."

His words brought an image to her mind, a totally forbidden image. Her clit swelled. She tried to maintain her cool composure, but when his middle finger found its way through her curls and sank all the way to the knuckle inside her heat, she gave up any pretense of control.

"Mmm, just look at you. Your cunt is ripe for the plucking. I think I'm going to really enjoy making you scream with pleasure."

When a second finger joined the first, her hips began to move, matching his pumping rhythm. After thrusting several times, Jackson brought both fingers all the way out. She wanted to beg him to come back, but her words died on her tongue as she watched him suck her juices off each digit.

"Tangy, but I'm going to need a little more to be sure." He spread her wide and dipped his head between her thighs and swept his tongue over her swollen clit.

She arched upwards, and he was there, holding her down with a hand splayed across her belly. She moaned and writhed under his assault. His tongue dipped in and out, tasting and sweeping her into a different realm. She went wild when he sucked her clit into his mouth and nibbled it. Once, twice, and she suddenly burst apart, shouting his name and flowing into his greedy mouth.

He stayed there for long seconds after her orgasm ended, relishing the little aftershocks. Then he lifted his head.

"Fucking beautiful," he murmured. "So fucking beautiful, baby."

Amen, was all she could think as she let her eyes drift closed. Then his weight lifted, and Grace opened them again, curious as to what he was about to do. She watched him standing beside the couch, an impressive erection tenting the front of his slacks and some unnamed emotion on his face.

He leaned down, kissed her forehead and murmured, "Sleep tight, pretty Grace."

Shock and mortification filled her as he walked to her door. As he turned the knob, she found her voice. "That's it?" She sat up and grabbed her blouse. "You're leaving?"

He winked at her. "The rest will be waiting for you in Vegas. If you want it, you'll have to come and get it."

As he opened the door and walked out, Grace saw red. "Vegas." Her mind was already churning with all the ways to make Jackson Hill squirm. "We'll just see who caves first."

Grace got up from the couch and went to the bedroom. She pulled on a pair of shorts and a tank top before heading to the phone. When she dialed her sister's number, her fingers still shook with anger.

"Hello?"

"He makes me crazy!" Grace shouted.

"Uh, Grace, it might help if you start by telling me who you're talking about."

Her sister's matter of fact tone never failed to calm her. "Jackson, He was just here."

"Jackson from work who has the hots for you? That Jackson? What was he doing at your apartment?"

Grace went to the kitchen and grabbed her chocolate bar from the fridge. "He said Merrick told him about my car accident and he wanted to know more about it."

"So he came to your apartment instead of waiting to ask you at work on Monday? There's something missing here. What's missing?"

Grace plopped onto the sofa and groaned. She could still smell his masculine scent. It was going to be a really long weekend. "Well, we sort of did more than talk."

"Oh, my God. Did you sleep with him?"

She felt her cheeks heat. Faith always seemed to have a way of making her feel like an unruly teenager. She tore open the chocolate bar and bit off a piece. "No, I didn't sleep with him. Although, I am a big girl. I'm allowed to have sex."

"Yeah, I know, but you're still my baby sister," she reminded her. "Okay, so, you didn't have sex. What exactly did you do?

"We, uh, we sort of made out."

"Was it horrible? Is he a crappy kisser?"

"He's not horrible. In fact he's so damn good my body is still humming."

"I just don't understand why you won't go out with him. It's clear you like him or you never would have let him touch you. Why are you holding back?"

There was the million-dollar question. "I don't know. He's smart, he works hard, he's a genuinely nice guy. Overbearing and annoying, but he's one of the good ones. Plus, he's hot as hell. My God, the things that man can do with his hands..." her voice trailed off as she remembered just exactly how talented he was with his fingers.

"Okay, so he's the best thing since Mom's double fudge brownies. Then what's wrong with him? Does he have like an extra nipple or something? What?"

Grace laughed. "No, he doesn't have an extra nipple."

"That's a relief," Faith said, her tone dripping with sarcasm.

Grace sobered as she thought over Faith's question. "I don't know, sis. He's just so intense. When I'm around him I feel like he can see right into my soul. I'm not sure I'm ready for a guy like Jackson."

"And yet you still made out with him. It seems to me like

your body is tired of your brain holding back. Maybe you need to give him a chance. See where it goes."

"I gave him a chance tonight and he left." Grace got angry all over again as she remembered his parting words. "Do you know what he said? He said if I wanted the rest, I'd have to get it from him in Vegas. See what I mean? He's so annoying."

"Vegas? Since when did you decide to go to Vegas?"

"Since today. There's a big IT convention there next week. Jackson invited me to come along and check out the latest technology for Vaughn's. When I refused, he called me chicken. Can you believe that?"

"Ah, the magic word. Boy, he really knows how to push your buttons."

Oh he'd pushed buttons all right. And she'd had a delicious orgasm as a result. "Yeah, don't remind me."

"So, maybe you go to Vegas. Maybe you see if you can't make *him* squirm a little."

Grace grinned. "I like the way you think."

"Thanks. Now, can I get back to my book? Rafe just tied Kimberley to the bed."

"Sure, but I want it when you're done."

"Of course."

They said their goodbyes and hung up. Grace bit off another piece of her chocolate bar and thought about Faith's words. Make him squirm. Now that's something she could wrap her mind around.

Chapter Five

"I have nothing to say to you."

Jackson was more confused than ever. He'd been going insane since he'd tasted her juices. Nothing in his life had prepared him for the sweet flavor of Grace Vaughn. The entire weekend had passed in a blur. His mind had lingered on the feel of Grace's soft curves, the intoxicating flavor of her arousal. He'd ached to take her, to drive his cock deep, fuck them both into the next damn century. Knowing she'd resent the hell out of him afterwards had caused him to hold back. He needed her to come to him.

As they sat on the plane at the Las Vegas airport waiting to exit, Jackson was at his wits end with Grace's refusal to speak to him. "What's your problem? You've been silent the entire plane ride."

"You know what the problem is. Don't play dumb."

"You're pissed I left you the other night, is that it? You think it was easy for me to walk away?"

"I think you're crazy if you think I'll ever let you so much as touch me again, much less do anything else on this trip."

"You would've hated me if I'd taken you to bed. You would've run so fast in the opposite direction my head would've spun. Then where would we be?"

Her gaze remained on the window as she said, "Your biggest problem is that you think you know me so well. You don't, so stop acting like you do."

"I know you well enough to know you weren't ready to sleep with me. You would've woken up cursing me. Don't deny it."

She swiveled around to face him. At least she wasn't avoiding him. It was something. "You know what I think? I think you're the one who's afraid. I think you like it when I turn you down, because then you don't have to deal with a woman who can string two words together. It's easier to date bimbos. There's no real challenge there."

"The women I date aren't bimbos, and you're purposely steering the conversation away from what's really bothering you. You wanted me, and I left."

Grace leaned closer and growled, "I wanted you, yes, but you can't handle a real woman. You like women who drop at your feet and fawn all over you. I've seen them, so don't deny it. Don't play the martyr, either. It doesn't suit you. You left because you got scared."

Jackson's anger rose. "You want it all out in the open? Fine, but don't blame me if it's more than what you wanted to hear." He lifted his hand and cupped the back of her head. When she tried to pull away, he held her firmly with a fist full of her soft blonde curls. His whisper was for her ears alone. "Fear isn't what has my cock rock hard right now. Fear isn't what rode me the other night, either, baby. I wanted to take you to the floor and fuck you. First I wanted to see you come again so I would have gotten on top of you and watched your pretty blue eyes dilate and your face flush with heat. But then I would have wanted to see your sexy ass. I would've flipped you over and fucked you from behind, maybe spanked you a few times for being so goddamn contrary. After we recovered a bit, I would have taken you to the shower and fucked you there too. I want my cock inside of you. Your mouth, your cunt, your ass. I want my come filling you. I left because I wanted you *too* much."

Her mouth dropped open and her face turned beet red.

Was she afraid of him now? Shit. This wasn't at all how things were supposed to go. "I'd never—" He never got to finish what he was about to say because the flight attendant came over the intercom and announced they could exit the plane. Their alone time had just disappeared.

Baggage claim and the cab ride seemed to take forever. When they arrived at the hotel, there wasn't any privacy to be had there, either. They checked in for the convention and retrieved their room keys. By the time they had a few minutes alone in the elevator, they'd arrived at their floor, and Grace scurried off to her suite, leaving him to wonder how things had gone from bad to worse.

He went to his own room, slid the keycard through the slot and pushed the door open. After tossing his suitcase on the bed, he looked around at the opulent room. A foyer led to a large living room. Off to his left was a little half-bath. The dark furniture, offset by bright carpeting and curtains, looked classy and comfortable. The big plasma flat screen was a nice touch. A mirrored wet-bar, cool. He made his way into the bedroom and noticed more mirrors, walls of them, in fact. Jackson stared at the bed and imagined making love to Grace on the luxurious linens. He groaned. He went around a corner and found the bathroom. Damn thing was fit for a king. The centerpiece was a deep Roman tub surrounded in black marble. Christ, he really wanted Grace in that tub. His cell phone rang, interrupting the X-rated movie playing in his head. He checked the caller ID, hoping it was Grace. His mom. Oh, yeah, he really wanted to talk to her. She'd see right through him, know something was wrong and want to help. It rang again. For a moment he thought of avoiding her. She'd only worry, though. Didn't matter that he was thirty-two.

"Hi, Mom."

"Hello, dear. Did your trip go okay?"

Just dandy if you consider alienating the one woman he was beginning to suspect he loved. "It was great."

"No problems checking in?"

"No, I'm good. How's Dad?"

"Apparently fine, considering he went golfing with your brother and hasn't been back all day."

He heard the disgust in his mother's voice. She wanted to coddle his dad now that he was beginning to slow down, but no one coddled Edgar Hill. The man thought he was indestructible. "Scott will see to it that Dad doesn't overdo." His brother, younger than him by two years, had always been able to get around their dad somehow. He was a little too good at manipulating people, which was probably what made him a really great sales rep.

"Enough about your stubborn father. How are you? You sound down. Is everything okay?"

And there it was, mother's intuition. He'd never been able to escape it, though he'd tried aplenty. "I think I may have wrecked things with Grace." He walked back into the bedroom and collapsed onto the bed.

"That girl you told me about the last time you were here visiting?"

He'd broken down and told his mother everything about Grace Vaughn. How beautiful she was when she smiled, how crazy she made him when she said something ornery to goad him. His mother had started to hear wedding bells, though, so he'd played it off.

168

"Yeah, that's the one."

"She went with you to the convention, right?"

What was his mother up to now? "Uh, right."

"You two will be there for three days?"

Jackson sat up. "We come back on Thursday. Why the twenty questions?"

"Well, seems to me you shouldn't be wasting time with me. Get off the phone and ask her to dinner."

"She pretty much hates my guts. I'm the last person she wants to break bread with, trust me."

His mother made a frustrated sound. "No she doesn't. She's just playing hard to get."

He laughed. "Women don't do that anymore."

"Some things may have changed over the years, but they haven't changed that much. Ask her to dinner. If she refuses, ask her again. And remember to be a gentleman about it, Jackson."

He chuckled as he stood. "Always."

"Don't be smart," she warned. "You aren't too old for me to box your ears."

They said their goodbyes, and Jackson went to the hotel phone and dialed Grace's room. She answered on the second ring.

"Hello?"

"Have dinner with me." He thought of his mother's advice and added, "Please?"

"I'm not hungry."

"Then watch me eat. Come on, Gracie, we need to talk."

Silence.

His gut knotted. "Grace?"

169

"Okay, give me twenty minutes to freshen up. I'll meet you in the lobby."

Jackson could have kissed his mother in that moment. "I'll come to your room," he said.

"The lobby, Jackson," she stated firmly.

Damn, the woman was too astute. If he'd picked her up at her room, he might have had a chance at another kiss...or more. "The lobby in twenty minutes," he confirmed.

They both hung up, and Jackson tried to figure out this new mood of Grace's. She'd been pensive, subdued. Wasn't that how murderers felt right before they cracked? Determination filled him. If Grace really was playing hard to get, then he'd just have to up the ante. After all, they were in Vegas and he had her away from her family, just as he'd wanted. Time to show his hand.

♦

"No, thank you. I'm just waiting for a friend." Grace was getting damned tired of having men assume she was for sale. Good lord, did the men in Vegas think *everything* was so easily bought?

The middle-aged stranger with the pot belly and receding hairline glanced at her breasts yet again, then licked his lips. "Are you sure? It'd be my pleasure to show you around the casino."

She pasted a smile on her face and pointedly stared at his wedding ring. "No, really, I'm not interested in—"

"The lady's with me."

Grace turned to see Jackson behind her, a fierce frown marring his brow. He looked ready to brawl. She was never so glad to see him. "I was just about to come find you."

Jackson placed his hand at the small of her back and waited until the stranger took the hint and disappeared into the hotel bar. "What an ass."

"You can say that again. And that was ass number three. The first two offered money."

His eyebrows shot up. "Jesus, are you serious?"

"Deadly serious. I didn't think the dress was that revealing, but maybe I was wrong."

Jackson looked her over and hummed his approval. "You look beautiful. Some men just don't know a lady when they see one."

She liked hearing the compliment. "Thank you. You don't look half bad yourself."

Half bad, yeah right. He was drop-dead gorgeous. Black Armani slacks and a white dress shirt, sleeves rolled up and open at the collar. His cropped espresso hair and the dangerous aura that seemed to be such a part of him only completed the package. She wanted to climb him like a great big mountain. A hard, hot, sexy mountain.

Grace fidgeted in her heels. She had all of two dresses, one red, one black. She'd decided to wear the black dress. It was a simple design hitting just above the knees. She'd wrapped her hair into a French twist and put on a little blush and lipstick. The heels weren't too high that she risked breaking her neck, but they weren't flats, either. The way Jackson kept looking at her legs, she figured she'd done okay with the clothes and shoes.

"So, where to?"

"I figured we'd keep it simple, eat here at the hotel. No worries about taxis that way."

"You called ahead and reserved a table?"

He nodded. "I've thought of everything," he murmured.

"Now why doesn't that surprise me?"

He chuckled and steered her toward a fancy restaurant. She was still so dazzled by all the glitter and lights. Vegas life and small town Ohio were not to be compared. It was as if she'd entered an entirely different world.

As the hostess seated them, Grace noticed they were tucked away in a private little alcove, away from the main part of the restaurant. She wondered if Jackson had planned that along with everything else. "Nicely secluded. Your idea?"

Jackson winked, and it did things to her. Wild things. Her pussy flooded with liquid heat and her heartbeat sped up. "I wanted to get you alone so we could talk. Is that a crime?"

Grace reached for her menu and held it in front of her, not bothering to answer. "The prices are outrageous."

"Everything in Vegas is outrageous," he said. "Answer me."

She dropped the menu and frowned. "No, it's not a crime. Happy now?"

He stayed silent, watchful and mysterious. Grace wished she had the ability to read Jackson's moods, but the only time she knew what went through his ornery mind was when he was turned on. In those heated moments when he teased, challenging her to take him up on his offer to push their relationship into more intimate territory, Jackson dropped his armor. Only then could she see into his soul. And what she observed made her nervous as hell. He wasn't an easy man. Jackson was hard, inside and out. He played hard, worked hard, and he expected everyone to do the same. Grace was very much afraid that he wanted things from her she didn't know how to give. The X-rated things he'd whispered to her on the plane had sent her straight to a cold shower. Well, a cold shower after she'd answered several phone calls from her family asking if she'd landed safely. Not just her mother, like normal people, but nearly the entire Vaughn bunch had called to make sure she hadn't crashed. She loved them, but there were times she was tempted to move to Alaska just to escape their coddling.

Crap. Three days in Vegas. Three days of denying Jackson and the needs he brought out in her. As if she was that strong.! She'd be lucky to last one night before she came begging for him to fuck her.

When their waitress came around and started her spiel about the house specials, Grace glanced across the table. The wicked look Jackson shot her way told her two things really quick. He knew exactly what she'd been thinking, and she'd be lucky if she could still walk by the time he finished with her. Excitement had her heart beating faster. Fear had her pretending an unusual interest in the menu.

Chapter Six

Jackson gritted his teeth in frustration. They'd long since finished their meals. Grace had eaten a damned grilled chicken Caesar salad, probably because it was the cheapest thing on the menu, while he'd devoured a succulent filet mignon. After the waitress had brought out the dessert cart, Jackson nearly came in his slacks as he watched Grace's deep blue eyes glaze over. She'd stared at the selection of rich culinary delights and licked her lips. He'd wanted to pull her out of her chair, slam her down on the table and have her pussy for dessert. But her refusal to pick anything from the cart was causing him to fast lose his patience.

"Get dessert," he ordered.

Grace played with her water glass and eyed the cart as if she wanted to steal away with the whole thing. "No, I can't. It's all just too expensive."

Christ, her cousin was the owner of the company she worked for and she still refused a simple slice of cake? "Merrick doesn't mind if we indulge ourselves a little when we're on business trips. He would insist if he were here, and you know it."

"I would feel like I was taking advantage of him. Just because we can turn in our expenses doesn't mean we should go hog wild."

Was she for real? Anyone else would be racking up the bill if they knew their boss was footing it. Damned irritant. "A slice of cake is not going hog wild. Having the entire cart would be hog wild." She shook her head and looked away. "Fine, then I'll pay for it. Just get the damned chocolate cake, Gracie."

Her lips thinned in anger. "I'm not poor. I don't need you buying me cake, Jackson Hill. I just don't want it. Let it go."

Jackson looked at the waitress and growled, "We'll take two slices of chocolate cake. Put it on my bill."

"Yes, sir," the waitress squeaked before rushing off.

He watched as Grace's nostrils flared with anger. "You did not just do that."

"Why do you refuse such a simple thing? There's no point, Gracie. And don't ever lie to me again. You want the fucking cake. Hell, you were damned near drooling over it."

"I decide what I want and don't want, Jackson, not you."

As the waitress came back carrying a tray filled with their cake, he was forced to silence. After she placed the decadent treats on the table then left, his gaze snagged on Grace. She licked her lips, but still didn't pick up her fork.

Jackson had had enough of her stubbornness to last a lifetime. He leaned across the table and whispered, "Baby, we can eat the cake here with forks and napkins like civilized adults, or we can lick it off each other back in my room. Your choice."

Grace didn't speak, but merely sat there, as if warring with herself. Was she imagining what he wanted her to imagine? Jackson desperately wanted an answer to that question. She shocked him when she picked up the fork and took a chunk out of the dark dessert. Her eyes were trained on him as she brought it to her mouth. The fork disappeared between her plump, ruby lips. She closed her eyes and moaned deep in her throat. When she went back for a second bite, Jackson spread his legs and sat back, content to watch Grace seduce him with chocolate. By the time she'd devoured the entire slice, his cock was hammer hard and ready to be buried deep inside Grace's pretty cunt. Tight and hot, right where he belonged for the next fifty years.

Grace sat back, dabbed her lips with the white linen napkin and murmured, "You're right. I did want the cake, but you were wrong about the other."

Jackson cleared his throat. "What other?" Hallelujah, he really could speak.

This time it was Grace's turn to lean across the table. "I never mix my two favorite vices. Chocolate is orgasmic all on its own. When I have sex, I prefer to leave the food out of it."

And again, Grace Vaughn takes the lead. Their verbal sparring matches were wearing him down. Jackson couldn't figure out why he didn't just forfeit, lay himself at her feet and beg her to put him out of his horny misery. He sure as hell wasn't getting anywhere by hoping she'd come to him on her own.

She smiled as the waitress brought their checks. Jackson could only sit there, staring like a horny teenager with his first nudie magazine. By the time they were headed out of the restaurant he had his voice back and his cock was only semi-erect. As they reached the elevator, he took her arm and turned her toward him. "Come up to my room for a drink."

"You aren't going to molest me, are you?"

Her soft smile as she looked up at him caused his gut to clench. Her sweet innocence was intoxicating. He could well understand why her family wanted to wrap her in cotton and set her on a shelf. On the other hand, he wanted nothing more than to show her all the dirty sex acts he'd learned over the years. Things that would leave them both gasping for air. The elevator dinged and opened. Another couple stood inside waiting for them to get on.

"Come on," he urged as he pulled her along beside him. The doors slid shut, sealing them in with the other two. The walls of the elevator were mirrored, and he was able to see the other couple behind them, kissing. Christ, that was all he needed, a visual aid.

Grace rose on her toes and whispered, "You're blushing."

Jackson's patience snapped. He cupped her chin and ground out, "Keep pushing me and you'll get more than a drink when we reach my room."

She tried to step away from him, but he had his hand wrapped around her forearm, preventing her escape. "I know better than that, Jackson. The other night is proof I have nothing to fear from you."

She just wouldn't let it go that he'd left her. Couldn't she see he'd done it for her own good? He could have stayed and made love to her the entire night. Hell, the entire weekend. He'd tried to give her time to accept him, to accept a relationship with him. All he'd done was make it worse. One step forward, ten steps back.

Jackson's gaze took in the tight black dress that accentuated her small breasts and slender hips. He imagined slipping her out of it. Inch by delicious inch. Would she be wearing panties this time? "We'll see," he murmured.

As the elevator stopped on their floor, he looked in the mirrored wall again. The couple had practically climbed each other. The woman's head was thrown back in rapture, and the man was in the process of nibbling his way down to the brunette's cleavage. Jackson peeked over at Grace, gauging her reaction to the pair of exhibitionists. Her eyes were round as quarters, but she wasn't looking away. He noticed her nipples were hard little pebbles beneath the black silk. She liked watching. Interesting.

He tugged on her arm to indicate the elevator had stopped. She cleared her throat and walked through the open doors, completely ignoring him. He ended up getting dragged along in her wake. Jackson couldn't tell if she'd decided to go to his room for a drink or not. He'd never seen her act so damned mysterious. When she turned right down the hall, which would take her to his room instead of left toward her own, he let out a breath, thankful he wasn't going to have to toss her over his shoulder and haul her cute ass to his suite by force. He was just desperate enough to do it.

He moved alongside her and let her pull her arm away. As they approached his suite, she stopped and adjusted her purse higher on her shoulder. "Drinks. Nothing more."

He moved to close the gap between them and let his fingers trail down her check. "Unless you want more."

"I don't."

Her voice wasn't quite as steady as it had been in the restaurant. Jackson had to hold back a triumphant grin. "Little liar."

She was about to say something more, something caustic, no doubt, but he took his keycard out of his pocket and slid it through the slot. He pushed the door open before stepping aside. "After you, Gracie."

Her nose shot in the air as she walked past him. He took in the sway of her hips and her tight, slightly rounded ass. God in heaven, the woman was a gift. Her body made his every instinct kick in. He wanted to slam the door shut and fuck her into submission. Force her to accept him as her lover—her only lover. Soon, he promised his overeager cock. Even in his lusty fog, he noticed there weren't any panty lines, but that wasn't enough proof. The only way he'd know for sure if she had anything on under the sexy dress was to get her out of it.

Jackson stepped inside the room and closed the door behind him, then flipped the security lock into place. As he hit the switch, illuminating the room, and moved toward her, Grace licked her lips, her posture stiff as a board. He could see the war going on inside her pretty head so clearly. She wanted him, but she wasn't happy about it. By the time they went back to Ohio, she would belong to him. The only other option was just too damned depressing to consider.

He went to the desk at the far side of the room and picked up the phone. "Champagne or wine?"

"Wine."

Jackson ordered a bottle of Merlot, then looked at Grace as an idea struck. "We're also going to need a deck of cards." He watched her frown at him from across the room. When he hung up, he said, "You've never played poker with me. Since we're in Vegas and all, I thought it seemed appropriate."

"Be warned. I've been playing poker since I was big enough to walk. My dad taught me. I'm not bragging when I say I'm good. In fact, poker helped pay for books and gas when I was in college."

"I know. I've seen you play with Blade and Merrick. You're very good. But so am I. What do you say to a few hands of five card stud?"

Grace went to the couch and sat. "Sure, why not? But you'd better not be a sore loser. I hate sore losers."

"Ditto, Gracie," he said. A knock on the door indicated room service. After taking the wine and cards, he tipped the guy and went to the chair next to the couch. He poured a glass of wine and held it out to Grace. When she took it, he poured another glass for himself. They were silent as they each took a sip. He set his on the coffee table and opened the box of cards. As he shuffled, he explained the rules. "Five card stud, nothing wild."

"Easy enough. Are we playing for money?"

"No, not money. Information."

"Huh?"

"If I win, you have to tell me three things about yourself. Good things, not like 'I like the color red.'. If you win, I have to tell you three things about myself. What do you say?"

She grinned. "You're going to be doing a lot of talking."

He didn't speak as he dealt. He waited for her to look at her hand. When she discarded two, he slid two new cards across the coffee table. She picked them up, but Jackson couldn't tell if she was happy or not. She was good at not giving herself away. He looked at his own cards and discarded one, then waited for her to show her hand. She had two pair, kings and deuces. All he'd ended up with was a pair of nines. He placed his own hand face up on the table and watched her expression change from blank to pure wickedness.

"Start talking," she demanded.

Shit, he'd wanted to find out more about *her*. He'd been sure he could beat her. Next time, he vowed.

"Let's see... I have a fondness for motorcycles. I always have. I have two that I keep at my brother's place. I can't stand movies with sad endings. They're a complete waste of time to me. Also, my mom has always wanted to go to Ireland, so my brother and I are pitching in and sending my parents there for their wedding anniversary next year."

"Ah, that's so sweet," she said, her face softening. "I bet she'll be thrilled."

"She'll probably get on us for spending so much money, but, yeah, she'll be pleased as hell too."

"Okay, my turn to deal." Grace scooped up the cards and started to shuffle. He'd seen her at work before, but her skill with a deck never failed to impress him. She dealt five cards each, then placed the deck in the center. He looked at his hand and had to stifle a grin. "I'll stay."

No expression from Grace as she picked up her cards and tossed one down and picked a new one up from the deck. She looked at him, and he laid his cards out face up. "Three aces."

Grace showed her hand. "That beats my lousy pair of fours."

"Three things. Start talking."

"I'm not that exciting, but okay. I collect snow globes. All sizes. Expensive ones, cheap ones. I just love snow globes. I enjoy old black and white movies. In fact, Bette   Davis is my favorite actress. Third fact. I hate food that's yellow. Corn, squash, bananas, I can't stand any of them."

He laughed. "What do you have against the color yellow?"

She played with the cards, shuffling in various ways. "I don't know, it's the strangest thing. I've just always hated yellow food."

Jackson held out his hand. "Give them over, my turn to deal." She placed the cards in his hand. Their fingers touched. Sparks jumped between them. "One more hand to break the tie," he murmured.

She cleared her throat and took a sip of her wine. "Just don't pout when I win."

Jackson dealt the cards. They both seemed to be on pins and needles, as if this last hand meant more to them both than merely breaking a tie. Or maybe he was just reading more into their game than what was there.

Grace threw away two cards, and he dealt her two more. He tossed down two of his own cards and took two more off the top of the deck. He watched as she showed her hand. Damn, a flush. He showed his own and growled, "Two pair. You win."

"Come on, I get three more Jackson facts."

"Yeah, yeah. Well, I'm a black belt in Karate. The only books I ever read are business related, though that dirty book in your apartment has me thinking I've been missing out on a lot."

"It's not dirty, it's romance."

He took a sip of his wine, draining the glass. "Last thing. I watch you walk when we're at the office. Not a day goes by that I don't stare at your ass."

Grace shook her head. "I'm not sure that qualifies as a fact."

He leaned across the table and whispered, "Do you care?"

Suddenly she stood and moved toward him, her steps precise. He couldn't read her mood now. "Not really," she stated, her voice so low he barely heard her.

Jackson stood too. His fingers stroked the baby-soft skin of her cheek. "What do you want?" Her mesmerizing gaze drifted over him, teasing him to full alert status. "Gracie?"

"This," she whispered, before rising to her toes and pressing her lips to his. She was gentle, shy, as if unsure what to do with him. When her tongue slid over his bottom lip in a curious perusal, he gave up any pretense at control. He enfolded her in his arms, pulling her against his body, fitting her curves to him. He thrust his pelvis against her lower abs, saying without words what he would demand from her if she continued her little game. She moaned against his mouth and dug her fingers into his hair, then brought one leg up to wrap around his waist. Jackson cupped her ass and lifted her off the floor, forcing her to clutch onto him with both legs.

He pried his lips from hers and gave her one last chance to walk away. "Be sure, baby. Be damned sure this is what you want."

Her breath came out in pants as she said, "You left me. I needed you, and you left me."

"Never again," he promised as he strode across the room. "I swear it."

"I'll knee you in the balls if you ever do that again, Jackson."

It wasn't until he entered the bedroom, flipped on the bedside lamp and sat on the end of the bed that her words registered. "I don't doubt it for a second," he murmured as he tasted her lips with his tongue. He coaxed her to open for him. When she surrendered, he delved inside, addicted to her sweetness. The flavor of her...there wasn't another woman on earth who tasted as sinfully sweet as Grace.

With her straddling him, Jackson's cock was so hard he was afraid he'd end up with an imprint of his damned zipper, but he was loath to let her up long enough to undress. She dipped her head and licked his neck, teasing and nibbling at his overheated skin. Her lower body gyrated against his. Jesus, the woman was hot. Sexy and hot and all his. He lifted away from her and grasped her waist, standing her in front of him. Grace's cheeks were flushed, her lips swollen. Several locks of hair had come loose from her twist. She looked ready to fuck. "You make me crazy, baby. But why the change of heart? Why now?"

"I decided I didn't want to deny myself anymore. I've wanted you for so long, Jackson. I don't know if that's a good thing or not, but I don't feel like questioning it tonight. I just want you to touch me."

"I'm going to do more than touch you, baby. A hell of a lot more." He smoothed his palms up her sides until he reached her breasts. He cupped them through the black silk of her dress. He let his thumbs tease the hard tips, and Grace swayed. He pulled his hands away and ordered, "Undress."

Grace didn't speak, though her expression conveyed all he needed to know. She was nervous. Excited, but still a little afraid of his sexual appetites. "Don't think so hard, baby."

"I'm not." They both knew she was lying, but he let it go and waited. She took a deep breath and moved her fingers to a hidden zipper along her right side. As she worked the straps off her shoulders, the dress fell free, landing in a black pool at her feet. His gaze went straight to her pussy. No panties. Oh, hell. His hand lifted, cupping her neatly trimmed mound. "Mmm, I missed this little pussy. I'm going to fuck it so hard."

"Jackson." His name came out as a pleading whisper, and it was music to his ears.

He leaned forward and placed a gentle kiss to her clit. "My dick is going to feel so good sliding inside of you." He reached behind her and unhooked her bra, his attention rapt as her breasts were bared for him. He leaned forward, unable to help himself, and tasted one turgid peak. Grace shuddered and tunneled her fingers in his hair. He swirled his tongue around the puffy areola before sucking as much as he could into his mouth.

"Yes, just like that," she breathed out. "Oh, God, that feels so good."

He pulled back and stared at her. "Take your hair down, Gracie," he commanded as he rose to his feet. He started unbuttoning and unzipping his slacks as Grace lifted her fingers to her hair. She pulled several pins free, letting them fall where they may. She shook the shiny strands out and finger combed them. In the dimly lit room, her hands now clasped together in front of her, Jackson thought she looked like a sweet angel. An innocent, untouchable being that he had no business breathing near, much less fucking. And if anyone would've attempted to keep him from her in that instant, he would've fought to the death to get to her. It didn't much matter that he was too old for her, too hard and too experienced. She was his, and he'd willingly shed blood to keep her.

Naked finally, he closed the few inches between them and cupped her cheek, her desire and trust clearly visible in her expression. His gut clenched. "I've wanted you here like this for so long. I have a lot of ideas. Dirty ideas. Things you've never considered doing, probably, but I won't hurt you. I'd never hurt you, Gracie."

She slid a hand between their bodies and wrapped it around his cock. "I may not be as experienced as you, but I'm not a little girl. I want to be here. It's my choice to be here with you."

The grasp she had on his dick seemed to prove her point rather well. "Have you ever played with bondage?"

She arched a brow. "You want to tie me to the bed?"

"Not quite, no." He stepped away from her, forcing her to release her hold on him. He'd been too damn close to coming. He went to his suitcase and pulled out a length of rope, holding it out for her to see. "I want to bind your breasts. Have you ever had a man bind you, baby?"

Grace's eyes widened. "You want to do what?"

He chuckled. "Don't look so scandalized. It doesn't hurt, I promise. You do trust me, don't you?"

She bit her lip and covered her breasts with her palms, as

185

if to protect them from his evilness. "I-I trust you."

"Prove it," he growled. "Come here."

Grace padded softly toward him, a frown creasing her brow. "I'm not into pain, so if you hurt me I'll make you pay for it later."

He tugged her hands away, then let his gaze take in the sight of her. Her nipples were pebble hard, her lips swollen from his kisses. "Pleasure, my pet, only pleasure."

"There you go with the pet thing again."

He leaned down and kissed the spot behind her ear, enjoying the little shudders his touch evoked. "You don't want to be my pretty little pet, Gracie?" He licked the shell of her ear and nipped at the delicate lobe. "Are you so sure of that?"

"Please, Jackson, you're making me crazy with this slow loving. I need you inside of me. Now, or I'll take matters into my own hands."

He lifted his head and smiled down at her. "First I'm going to bind you, *pet*, then I'm going to fuck you. After we've recovered, I'm going to show you something else I've been dying to do to you since the first time we met. Any objections?"

"Just one."

Shit, he hadn't expected that. "What?"

"Quit talking and fuck me," she ordered.

The woman definitely had a way with words. He grinned. "Yes, ma'am."

Chapter Seven

She'd let herself fall. It was that simple. She'd been so strong, resisting him, pretending to remain angry over his hasty departure in her apartment. The truth had smacked her in the face the instant she'd entered his suite. She'd known the only reason she'd let him talk her into a nightcap was because she knew where it would lead and she'd *wanted* it to lead there.

Jackson's fingers trailed over her nipples and she nearly came standing up. He moved around her until he was at her back, then he wrapped a length of the rope around her torso, just below her breasts. Grace grabbed his hand. "I'm not sure about this."

He cupped her breast as he held the rope in place with the other hand. "Don't be so suspicious, baby. You've known me a little over a year. I don't hurt women."

"But this is—"

"Different," he inserted as he pinched her nipple. Grace arched her back, unable to contain the whimpers. "So pretty. So soft and pretty. Let yourself experience something different, Gracie. If you hate it, I'll untie you."

Grace still didn't see the pleasure part of the whole binding thing, but Jackson seemed to think she'd enjoy it. Her sexual history wasn't extensive, not by a long shot, but neither was it dull. She'd enjoyed playing in the bedroom. Still...bondage?

She'd never even fantasized about having her breasts bound. Tied to the bed and being ravished by Jackson, now that was a fantasy she could sink her teeth into.

"You're doing it again," he whispered against her ear a second before nipping the lobe with his teeth. She felt the little sting clear to her clit. "Sometimes sex doesn't make sense. There's not always a reason as to why it feels good. I know what I'm doing. I'm not a novice here."

When he slung both ends of the rope over her shoulders and they landed between her breasts, Grace clenched her hands at her sides to keep from yanking it away. Next Jackson ran both ends of the rope under her breasts, then brought them over her shoulders again. After he brought it around her once more, just above her breasts, creating a sort of crisscross harness with the rope, she started to understand why he wanted to do this with her. Her breasts were squeezed between the lengths of rope. It put them on display in a way she'd never seen. As Jackson tightened the rope, she had to clench her thighs together. Her pussy flooded with liquid warmth, and her breasts felt suddenly very swollen and sensitive. Jackson slid his thumb over one and her clit throbbed with need. "Oh, god," she groaned.

"Is it too tight?"

She could barely talk, she was so far gone. "No," she breathed out.

Jackson moved around to her front. He was so big, so powerful, she felt dwarfed next to him. Small and vulnerable. She eyed his heavy erection, and her temperature spiked higher. He was huge, bigger than any man she'd ever been with. Grace licked her lips as she imagined sucking the round, purplish head into her mouth, teasing him to completion with her tongue, swallowing his hot come.

"Just look at you, baby. Your pale skin and hard, berry nipples." He plucked one, and her legs shook. "Are you sensitive? Do they need my mouth, pet?"

She nodded, unable to concentrate on anything besides the need to feel Jackson covering her breasts with his lips and tongue.

He took her by the hand and brought her to the bed, then instructed her to sit on the edge. He knelt between her thighs and, with their gazes locked, leaned forward and licked her nipple. Grace moaned and grasped his broad shoulders a second before he sucked the tip into his mouth.

"Jackson, oh, god, that feels..." She couldn't put her feelings into words. There were no words to describe what Jackson was doing to her.

He hummed against her skin as he plucked at her other turgid peak. Her body arched, needing him to fill her, to take her down and slide into her aching pussy. It was crazy to want another person so much. Later, she'd worry about what that meant, for now she couldn't think, could barely hang on for the ride.

Suddenly Jackson pulled his lips away. She desperately wanted to beg him to come back, but he cupped her mound and stroked her slit with his middle finger, causing her to sink into oblivion a little more.

"Your pussy is so wet, I could feed on you for hours, baby. Would you like that? Do you want me to tongue-fuck you?"

Her answer was to place her hand over his and push his finger inside her a little more. She spread her thighs wider, giving him better access to her aching cunt. Jackson reached around her body with his other hand, grabbed the rope harness and tugged, squeezing her breasts tighter. He dipped his head and licked a lazy circle around her nipple. Several torturous circles, and she started to plead. "Jackson, please, suck it."

He leaned back, his eyes glittering silver pools in the dimly lit room. "Are you my pet?"

She knew what he wanted. Total submission. For Jackson, nothing else would do. "I'm your lover," she answered, unwilling to give him more power over her than he had already.

He grinned. "Soon you'll let me *own* you. You'll beg for it."

Nothing. Not a single smart ass retort. Of course, when his mouth fastened onto her nipple and his teeth grazed it lightly, she forgot all about one-upsmanship and let herself enjoy Jackson's passion. He pushed her back on the bed and rose over her, his entire length pressed against her. As his mouth journeyed down her body, Grace dug her fingers into his hair. When he reached her pussy, Grace propped her feet on the mattress and spread herself open for him. A muscle in his jaw jumped wildly, and she heard him emit a low groan before dipping between her thighs and suckling her clit.

"Jackson," she cried out, her fingers digging deeper, holding him against her.

Jackson wrapped his arms around her thighs and speared her entrance with his tongue. Her lower body shot off the bed.

"Touch your pretty tits, baby. Let me see you play with your sensitive little nipples while I eat this juicy cunt."

Grace was well beyond denying him. She forced herself to release his head and cupped her breasts in both hands. Her nipples were so sensitive, even her own touch had her rioting out of control. Jackson's intense gaze stayed on her as he lapped up her cream.

He was so close to coming, he could barely restrain himself. He wanted to be snug inside Grace's slim, delicate body, pounding deep. He wanted her to remember this trip. Every time he looked at her, she'd remember the rope around her breasts, the teasing torture of his tongue inside her cunt, the way their bodies fit so perfectly together as he knew they would.

As she played with her nipples, driving them both crazy, Jackson suckled her clitoris. Her plump nether lips and the slippery slit between made him hungry. "If I don't get more of that honey, I'll surely die, Gracie."

He lowered his head and licked her from her clit to her dewy lips then in between, lapping up her delicate cream. Her legs started to close around his head, but his hands clutched her, holding her firmly in place. Jackson tasted her tangy flavor on his tongue and knew he'd never sampled anything sweeter. He inhaled her womanly scent, sucked her clit between his teeth and nibbled.

Grace's hands flew to his head, clutching and grasping handfuls of his hair. The sting, had him releasing her and demanding, "Put your hands back on your tits. Don't make me spank them."

Her gaze narrowed on him. "You wouldn't dare."

He released one of her thighs and delivered a gentle slap to her breast. Grace arched off the bed.

"Fuck!"

Jackson took in her stunned expression. "Did that hurt, pet?" He knew it didn't. Her breasts were overly sensitive because of the binding. The slap would only stimulate them more.

"N-no, not exactly."

Jackson slapped her breast two more times, then switched to the other and paid the same attention to it. By the time he was through, Grace was writhing atop the mattress, her fingers clutching the bedspread above her head. Her juices soaked her thighs. He'd never seen a prettier sight.

"You're the sweetest vision, baby. I could spend months fucking this body."

When his tongue thrust between her folds this time, Grace lost it completely and pushed against his face, undulating as he tongued her. Pushing her shapely legs wide, he dipped his tongue into her hot opening several more times, luxuriating in the wild sounds coming from her throat. Grace's hands went to his head, grasping at his scalp and pushing his face against her. This time he let her get away with the little bit of insubordination. Jackson sucked at the tiny bundle of nerves and flicked back and forth, inciting another series of moans from Grace. When he used his teeth to tug on her clit, she flung her head back and came, shouting his name in untamed abandon.

A few more licks and she strained against the unyielding hold his hands had on her soft thighs. He reveled in her unrestrained passion as she seemed to try to hold onto the delirious feelings riding her body.

Jackson kept his tongue and lips against her sopping wet mound while she regained control. As she collapsed, the muscles in her thighs going slack and falling open, her hands dropped back to the mattress. Jackson lifted away and stood beside the bed, staring down at the tempting picture she presented. She appeared nearly asleep already, exhausted from her climax, but when he dipped his finger into her slippery cunt to gain her attention, her gaze flew to his. He pulled it out and brought it to her lips, rubbing her lube against them before he leaned down and kissed it off her. She whimpered and wrapped her arms around his neck, pulling him down until their bodies were aligned. As her breasts came into contact with his chest, he caught himself and stopped.

"This won't be a one-nighter, baby," he vowed.

"Don't," she warned. "I'm not promising forever."

Her refusal to give them a chance at a relationship burned. Jackson pressed his cock against her entrance. "At least give me more than this one night."

She arched a brow. "Negotiating?"

Jackson slid a finger over the rope binding her breasts. "I think you feel more than a passing attraction toward me, or you never would have let me tie your pretty tits. Admit it, pet."

Grace bit her lip and wiggled her hips, teasing the head of his cock. "It's more than a passing attraction. Now stop talking and put that cock where it can do us both some good."

Jackson moved away and left the bed.

"Hey!" she shouted. "Where are you going?"

He chuckled as he picked up his pants.

Grace rose on one elbow and pointed at him. "I swear, if you leave me again I'll strangle you in your damned sleep."

He grabbed a condom out of his pocket and waved it in her direction.

"Oh," she mumbled and fell back on the bed.

He quickly donned the condom, then placed his knee on the end of the mattress and crawled up her body. Stretched out on top of her, Jackson admitted, "Wild horses couldn't pull me away from you right now."

He rose to his knees between her thighs and hooked her legs over his arms. As he pushed his cock just inside her entrance, Grace groaned. It was just the smallest amount, but he watched closely as she chewed at her lower lip. She was so damned tight and small. He wanted to drive into her, slam his hips against hers and fuck her into the damned mattress. But Grace was too soft for that sort of rough sex. He needed to loosen her up or he'd risk hurting her.

"Stop biting that pretty lip, baby." He let go of her thighs and leaned down to lick at the wound she'd created with her nipping teeth. Slowly, careful of her size, Jackson began rocking his hips back and forth. He controlled his every motion, waiting for her tight opening to accommodate his intimate invasion. It wasn't easy, not when all his instincts were screaming at him to thrust hard and fast and deep, to fuck her the way he'd always imagined. But for Grace, he would bring nothing but sweet pleasure. For her, he'd push his own desires down. He'd do anything if it meant hearing that sexy sigh of satisfaction coming from her sweet lips again.

"You're so fucking tight," he murmured. "You feel amazing hugging my cock."

"You're...big," she managed as she gripped his shoulders.

"Mmm, flattery, Gracie? I had no idea you were capable." He kissed his way over her face to her neck where he found that same jumping vein that he'd tasted before, and bit down. Grace groaned and began to move her hips, building a slow rhythm. Jackson was bigger and a whole lot stronger. He easily held her still, keeping her from hurting herself.

"Not so fast," he warned. "We have all the time in the world." He continued his assault on her tempting pulse.

"I want fast, Jackson. Fast is good."

The sound of her anxious voice made him draw back. He had to grit his teeth against her appeal, but he wouldn't be cajoled. "No. Slowly this first time, or I could hurt you." To his horror, he saw a tear trickle down the side of her cheek. He kissed it away. "Next time you can run the show. You can go as wild as you want, I swear to God."

"I'm holding you to that."

He leaned down and kissed her. She capitulated finally, relaxing her flexing hips. "Two can play the torture game, you know," she warned.

He pictured Grace teasing him into a horny stupor. He swore. "I'll never live through it."

He resumed his slow, torturous movements, taking his time, needing to make it as pleasurable as possible. He feasted at her gorgeous tits, intent on building her passion. Jackson's temperature spiked when her inner muscles relaxed for him and he moved into her another inch. Her pussy held him in the tightest fist, and it was too much. Jackson lost it.

He pushed inside of her hard, watching as Grace's eyes shot wide with pleasure-pain. His mouth came down on hers, swallowing her cries with his kisses, turning pain into desire in an instant. Soon, their bodies were fused together, moving in unison. Jackson braced himself on his elbows on either side of her head and watched as her breasts moved with each thrust, her neck arched, her mouth dropping open. He pushed as deep as he could possibly go, then pulled out all the way and drove into her again, hard and fast.

"Fuck me, please," she begged him. "Harder, Jackson. Fuck me harder."

She wrapped her sleek legs around his hips, holding him in her sweet embrace, sending him over the edge and straight into a wildfire. He drove into her pussy one last time and came, hot jets that he wished he could fill her with, mark her forever. In that moment he'd never resented a condom more. Her body pulsed all around his cock, sucking him in farther, milking him dry. Grace collapsed, sated and exhausted.

"Oh, god, that was so worth the wait," she admitted, a dreamy smile curving her swollen lips.

He very nearly crumpled on top of her, but, mindful of her smaller size, he rolled to keep from crushing her. Jackson worried she'd be sore, it was clear she'd never been with anyone of his size. He had an overpowering need to comfort her, to ensure she had nothing but pretty memories of her first time with him.

Jackson slid out of her boneless body and went to the attached bathroom to dispose of the condom. He grabbed a washcloth, ran warm water over it and brought it to Grace. Her eyes were closed and she had a blissful smile on her lips. His body burned at the sight of her thorough exhaustion. As he bent down and pressed the cloth to the juncture of her thighs, her eyes flew open and her mouth formed a startled O. Neither of them spoke as he cleaned and soothed her sore flesh. Next he removed the rope and massaged her tender skin, paying special attention to the pink flesh of her breasts. As he slid into bed beside her and pulled her pliant body up against him, he felt her start to move. Jackson held her firm.

"Going somewhere?"

"I should get back to my own bed. We do have the conference to think about, you know."

"Stay. Please."

She hesitated a moment, but when she finally lay down next to him, his heart swelled. He pulled her close, wrapping his larger body protectively around her smaller one. She wiggled against him, pushing her soft, round bottom against his groin. The cleft of her ass created the perfect cradle for his dick, and he had to bite back a groan. She wiggled a little more, and he clutched her hip in one hand to hold her still. "There really are a lot of mirrors in these bedrooms, huh?" she mumbled, her voice drowsy, only half aware.

"Yeah. At first I thought it would be exciting to watch you in them while I fucked you, but I was too busy watching you to pay any attention to the mirrors." She fidgeted some more, and Jackson growled, "Enough, or I'm going to fuck this hot little ass too."

"Mmm, you don't have it in you. You're too old for that sort of exertion."

He swatted one cheek. "I'm going to love it when you have to eat those words, *pet.*"

"Promises, promises," she breathed. Seconds later, she was snoring.

Jackson smoothed her hair away from her cheek and kissed her. Damn, he couldn't let her go now. Convincing her they belonged together wasn't going to be easy, though. His cock stirred to life as she pushed more firmly against him. He had to bite back a curse. Sleeping wasn't going to be easy, either. Somehow he'd have to figure out a way to do both.

Chapter Eight

As Grace came awake, her senses tuned into her surroundings and she frowned. A warm male body lay plastered against her back. Oh, no, Jackson. In a wave of images, the night before came crashing in on her. The nightcap. The sex. The rope. Oh God, the rope. Her breasts tingled as she thought about the sensation of being bound. She already wanted to do it again. How messed up was that?

One dinner together and she'd flung all her convictions to stay away from the handsome man right out the window. She could blame it on the city. Vegas was known as Sin City, for a reason, right? Hell, she could even blame it on Jackson and his talented seduction. There wasn't a woman on the planet who would fault her. But it wouldn't be the truth. The truth smacked her in the face like a Mack truck. She'd fallen. Head over heels fallen. She wasn't even sure when it had happened. Probably the day her face had gotten in the way of his basketball game after they'd first met. His sexy grin and devilish good looks were enough to make any woman melt. Observing—and fighting—him this past year had sealed her fate. Still, he didn't have to know. Just because she was in love with the man didn't mean it needed to become public knowledge.

As delicately as possible, Grace lifted Jackson's arm from around her waist and slipped silently from the bed. She took two steps before he shifted, turned onto his stomach and started snoring. Grace watched him sleep, indulging in a rare moment of having Jackson off guard. Awake, he was a force to be reckoned with. Asleep, he seemed almost tender. He moved his leg, and the sheet fell away, giving her the perfect view of his naked ass. God, no wonder she'd fallen so fast. Who could possibly hold out against all that tanned, muscled flesh? *Move your butt, Grace, he'll be awake soon.* Her inner voice just didn't seem to understand the joys of looking at Jackson in repose.

Grace tiptoed to her dress, which was now a crumpled mess on the floor. She picked it up and slipped it on, then located her shoes. It took longer than expected to find both heels. She'd kicked one off at the end of the bed, but the other had slid beneath it. Shoes in hand, Grace sneaked out of the bedroom, grabbed her purse and rushed out the door, and smacked into a man in his pajamas. "Sorry," she muttered.

He grinned as he looked her over. "No problem. Really."

Grace grimaced as she imagined what she looked like. Sex, that's what. It was probably tattooed on her damned forehead. She tried to muster up some shame, but it just wasn't happening. The sex had simply been too good to wish it'd never happened. In fact, she was hoping the memories would sustain her for the rest of her life, because she sure as hell wasn't going back for a repeat performance. It was too dangerous to her heart to go anywhere near Jackson Hill. He should come with a warning sign or something.

Grace quickly fled down the hall to her own room. When she came to her door, it took her a ridiculous amount of time to find her keycard. She finally located it beneath a pack of tissues and slid it into the lock. As she stepped inside her room, she finally let herself breathe. Then it all hit her at once, and she slumped to the floor. What had she been thinking? She should have known she wouldn't be able to go on this trip and still keep her heart intact. But he'd wanted a relationship. Hadn't he said that last night? He was offering more than sex, so why was she so afraid? Because she knew Jackson. He'd sleep with her for awhile, it'd be great, then he'd be ready to move on to his next conquest. Her constant refusal to go out with him had posed a challenge. He liked a challenge. As soon as he had her tied around his little finger, she'd be out the door faster than a video game at Christmas time.

Her phone rang. Right away she knew who would be on the other end. She stood and went to it, staring as it rang again. "You can't hide forever," Grace muttered. "Be an adult and answer the damn thing." She ordered her hand to pick up the receiver when it rang a third time.

"Hello?"

"Chicken."

That single word uttered in Jackson's sleepy morning voice had the power to push her out of her self-recrimination. "I needed a shower," she hedged.

"You were running," he teased. "Don't lie."

She went to the couch and plopped down. "I wasn't running, I was walking."

"Why are you so afraid of me? Am I so terrible, Gracie?"

For the first time since meeting the overbearing man, Jackson actually sounded unsure of himself. She didn't want that. She wasn't sure what she wanted, exactly, but she didn't want him thinking things that weren't true. "I'm not afraid of you," she told him. "I'm afraid of the way you make me feel. I'm afraid of a relationship with you."

"Why, baby?" Jackson asked, his voice as warm and tempting as fresh baked cookies. "I'd never hurt you. You must know that by now. There's nothing to fear."

Oh, god, this was too cruel. It was like standing a little girl outside the gates of Disney World then telling her she couldn't go in. "I'm just a simple woman with a smartass attitude. I'm not up to your speed, Jackson. We both know it. You just refuse to see it."

"Get real. You're smarter, sassier and sexier than any woman I've ever met. You've all but flayed me alive with that wicked tongue of yours, so don't act like we aren't in the same league."

"We have a conference to attend," she said, hoping to derail him. "This has to end. I enjoyed last night, but it won't happen again."

Silence greeted her. When a loud knock sounded on her door, she dropped the phone. She left the couch to peek through the hole in the door. Her heart nearly stopped beating and her hands shook. Jackson. She bit her lip and turned the knob, knowing she shouldn't. Knowing he would only turn her inside out all over again. Jackson moved faster than she expected, stepping inside her suite and shoving the door closed behind him. He slammed her against the wall with all the force of a man who was through being polite.

"Bullshit it won't happen again," he bit out. "It's going to happen, I can promise you that. Over and over, baby. So many times you'll want to stay in my bed just to make it easier on the both of us."

"In your dreams," she shot right back. A split second later, he captured her lips with his, effectively shutting out all else. Their tongues mated, and just that fast she went down in flames. Glorious, hot, wonderful flames. They engulfed her, and she forgot her reservations, her worries of never having his whole heart. Suddenly her body was reminded of just how truly wonderful it felt to be loved by Jackson Hill. She hadn't really

201

needed the reminder, but as she slid her arms around his neck and sank into the kiss, she knew it didn't matter. Nothing mattered save for his taste. He picked her up and took her to the bedroom. They fell onto the bed together, rolling until she sprawled on top of him.

He broke the kiss and whispered, "I promised you could go wild, remember?"

"I remember." She wasn't sure what to do, though. She sat astride him, looking at him with his arms behind his head, a grin curving his sexy lips, and Grace suddenly felt vulnerable and unsure. Two things that usually had sarcastic comments spilling out of her mouth. For once, she had nothing to say. She could only stare at the male perfection stretched out beneath her.

Jackson reached up and cupped her cheek, sliding his thumb over her bottom lip. "Take off your dress, baby."

Right, lose the clothes, good idea. She forgot about the zipper this time and yanked the black material over her head. After tossing it to the floor, Grace cupped her breasts and squeezed. "I can still feel the rope against my skin. My nipples tingle when I think about it."

Jackson leaned forward and wrapped his powerful arms around her upper body. He placed a gentle kiss to each hardened tip. "I woke and you were gone, pet. The next time I bind you, I'm going to spank these pretty tits until they're nice and pink."

The use of that hated nickname should have doused her desire, but all it did was send her into a whirlwind of lust. God help her, she liked the idea of being his pet. At least in the bedroom.

"I think I'd rather tie you up instead. Have you ever been tied to the bed, Jackson?"

"No," he stated firmly. "The rope is for you, not me."

She frowned. "Speaking of rope... How did you manage to get that through airport security?"

He smoothed his palms over her ribcage, then down to her thighs. "I didn't want to chance it. I can just see explaining that one." They both laughed. "No, I bought it after we arrived."

Grace's blood ran hot in her veins when Jackson let his fingers journey toward her clit. He stopped short of touching her where she needed him the most, which made her crazy. As she braced herself on his chest, his words hit her. "Wait, you're telling me you went out and bought rope?"

"No, I called down to the desk."

"You can't be serious."

"This is Vegas, baby, they'll get you damn near anything for a price." He winked. "Now, can we please talk about the rope later?"

His fingers came dangerously close to her mound again, but not close enough. Grace wanted to beg him to touch her pussy, to put her out of her misery. She wouldn't, though, not this time. She was determined to make *him* plead a little for a change. Smoothing her fingertips over his muscular pecs and on down to his six-pack abs, Grace knew she'd never get enough of touching him. He was so big, so strong. She felt safe with him. As she came to the waistband of his black boxers, she laughed.

"What's so funny?"

"I can't believe you walked through the hotel in your underwear."

"It was only the hall, no one saw." He swatted her thigh and ordered, "Lift up so I can take them off. They're becoming a nuisance."

Who was she to say no? Grace lifted to her knees and let Jackson skim out of the only thing keeping her from her goal. He tossed them to the end of the bed and pulled her down until his cock was aligned with her pussy. "Mmm, much better." He started to move back and forth, rubbing against her swollen clit. She already wanted to feel him buried deep, but there was something else she craved even more.

She clenched her thighs tight. "Not so fast, big guy. I'm running this show, remember?"

He stopped and frowned up at her. "Just trying to move things along. You seem a bit slow this morning."

"I haven't had my coffee," she whispered as she licked his chest. The flavor of his warm, male skin had her suddenly ravenous for more. She trailed kisses down his torso, tasting and licking as she went. She lifted off him and lay down between his legs, eye level with his cock. It was huge. Veins traveled the engorged length, and a drop of moisture dripped from the slit in his tip. She dipped her head and lapped it up, tasting his salty male essence. "I've wanted to do this for so long. You have no idea how much I've wanted to do this."

She heard him emit a low growl in his chest, then his fingers grabbed handfuls of her hair. He pushed his hips upward and ordered, "Suck it, pet. Take me to heaven."

Grace wrapped a fist around the thick base. Her fingers weren't anywhere near touching. She opened her mouth and sucked the bulbous head into her mouth and swirled her tongue around once, twice, before teasing the tempting slit again. She heard him curse and push her head down a little more, as if determined to fill her mouth with his cock. Grace opened wider, eager to suck him deep, but she could only take in half of him before she started to gag.

At once Jackson pulled back. "You don't have to, baby. It's

okay."

Suddenly, Grace needed to please him. To show him she could match him, in bed and out. It seemed imperative to show him she was as capable of making him burn the same way he so easily sent fire licking through her veins. She let herself relax, enjoying his salty heat, licking and suckling the head. She opened again and sucked him in. His fingers flexed in her hair. His feral expression as she took another inch inside had shivers of awareness running down her spine. His jaw flexed as he watched her play with his cock, teasing and tasting. She pulled him out all the way and licked the entire length. He groaned, and his fingers tightened a little more, pulling almost painfully now. Grace took him deep again, this time swallowing his entire length.

"Fuck, yes," he growled. "That's the way. Swallow that cock, pet."

Grace hollowed her cheeks and sucked hard. Jackson cursed and pulled her head backward. She released him with an audible pop. He wrapped his own hand around hers at the base of his cock and rubbed the head back and forth over her lips.

"I've imagined you like this. You have no idea how many times I jacked off in the shower thinking of your pretty blonde head buried between my legs, baby."

Grace licked her lips, enjoying his sticky male fluid. She opened again, ready to suck him into her hungry mouth, but he held her away.

"Taste my balls. Let me watch you lick them, Gracie."

Grace's pussy flooded with liquid heat at the guttural words. As she dipped her head to the heavy sac beneath his rock hard length, Jackson hummed his approval. At the first swipe of her tongue his hips shot off the bed.

"Christ, yes."

Grace thrilled at the notion that she could drive him so completely wild. It fueled her desire to bring Jackson pleasure. She'd never been that into the act of fellatio, but with Jackson it was almost better than having him buried inside of her. Almost.

She cupped his balls and sucked as much of the tender orbs into her mouth as she could, licking and teasing, before she released them and drew his cock to her mouth again. She brought his tip between her lips and flicked it with her tongue.

"Damn, baby, that's enough," he said as he urged her off him. "I'm too close to filling that hot little mouth with my come."

"I wouldn't mind," she said softly.

He smiled at her and shook his head. "Soon, pet, but not now. Right now I have something else in mind." He lifted to a seated position, grasped her around the waist and pulled her onto the mattress beside him. "Turn over, on your stomach."

Grace didn't need to be asked twice. She turned and stretched out, waiting for him to make his next move. When he left the bed, she swiveled around. "Where are you going?"

"Stay put," he ordered as he leaned down and kissed the base of her spine. "I need supplies. I'll be right back."

He disappeared into the bathroom. Several seconds went by before he reappeared carrying a bottle. She knew that bottle. It was her hand lotion. Confused more than ever, she asked, "A massage?"

"No. Although I wouldn't mind giving you a full body massage." He waved the bottle in the air. "This is for lubricant. The best I could do on such short notice."

Her suspicions rose. "Uh, what are you planning to lubricate?"

He placed the bottle on the bed next to her, then sat on the edge. His hand smoothed over her ass, his gaze holding hers captive. "You can't guess?"

"You want to...back there?"

He dipped a single finger between her ass cheeks. "I want to fuck you back there, yeah."

"I don't know, Jackson."

"You've never been touched there, have you, baby?"

She snorted. "Of course not. Not all guys are as depraved as you."

His finger slid over her anus as he whispered, "You like my depravities, though."

"That's just what I let you think." It would have sounded better had her voice not quivered.

He dipped his finger inside the forbidden hole, and they both groaned. As he came over the top of her, pushing her legs apart and settling between them, Grace just barely had the presence of mind to put up a token protest. "This isn't something I'm comfortable with."

Jackson smoothed both hands over her buttocks. "You weren't sure about the rope, either, but that didn't turn out so bad, right?"

"The rope is different." His warm palms parted her, and she could well imagine him staring at her there. Her face heated. "Jackson, please don't."

"Ah, sweet Gracie, don't you know I only want to bring you pleasure? Let me have this virgin ass, baby. You'll see it's not as bad as you're imagining." He reached for the bottle, but she got to it first. She picked it up and held it out of his reach. "What is it? Are you afraid it'll hurt?"

"You only want to possess me. That's what this is about. Total submission."

"Yes, that's part of it. I want to make you mine, completely mine. The thought of other men touching you makes my gut burn as if I'd downed a bottle of acid. But there's more to it than that. I want you to surrender to me. Give me your trust, baby. You won't be sorry."

Grace knew she could be making the biggest mistake of her life. He could crush her heart as no one else could. She wouldn't be able to recover if Jackson destroyed her. But it was time to take a leap of faith. All this chemistry had to lead somewhere. Hell, he couldn't just be scratching an itch. She wouldn't believe that. She had to trust that he felt something for her.

She took a deep breath and handed him the lotion.

Chapter Nine

He'd known the instant he'd woken to find her gone that what he felt for Grace went deeper than lust. He was in love with her. The confounding woman damn near drove him to drink at times, but then she also made him feel whole, as if a piece of himself had been missing and he just hadn't known it. As he stared down at her stretched out on her stomach, trusting him with something precious, he wanted to howl it at the moon, shout from the highest mountain that Grace Vaughn belonged to him. No other had a right to touch her. Her soft cries and naughty glances were for him alone. He knew half the reason he was about to take her anally was because he wanted to fill every part of her, to imprint himself on her in a way that spoke of pure, animalistic ownership. He'd never needed another woman's total submission before. Hell, he'd never even asked. But with Grace, nothing less would do. He wanted her completely, with no barriers between them.

Jackson popped the top of the bottle of lotion and poured some into the palm of his hand. He smoothed his hands together, warming the fragrant liquid, before he stroked Grace's baby-soft skin. She moaned as he gently massaged her, readying her for the invasion of his cock where no man had ever been. The thought tore a growl from his chest.

He smoothed his fingertips over her lower back. "Your skin

is so delicate, baby. I could bruise you so easily."

"Mmm, I don't think I care with you doing that. Oh, my, that feels so incredible. You are one talented man, Jackson. I think I've died and gone to heaven."

His chest swelled with pride. He let his fingers drift over the small indentations above her bottom and murmured, "You are being a very good little pet, Gracie. Shall I reward you?"

"Please reward me," she moaned.

Jackson let his slick fingers dip between her ass cheeks and slid one digit up and down her anus. Over and over again, making certain she was completely slick with the vanilla-scented cream before he wiggled it into the tight pucker a bare inch. Her startled intake of breath at the tiny invasion reminded him that she was new to anal sex. He forced his raging libido down, hoping to build the pleasure slowly.

"Will you beg for me, pet?" The need to fill her with his cock instead of his finger began to ride him hard.

Her body, once so pliant, now seemed strung tight. "I don't know what you want. Please, you're making me crazy."

Her husky voice nearly did him in. "You know exactly what I want. Admit you're mine, baby, tell me now before I fuck this tight little ass."

"Oh, god, this is so insane," she cried out.

"Say it, Gracie."

She turned her head and glared at him. "Fine, I'm yours, happy now?"

He grinned. "For now." He pulled his finger free and poured more cream onto his fingers, then spread it around. "When my cock slides into this sexy little butt, it'll feel so incredible you'll come back for more. You'll crave this type of lovemaking after I'm through, I promise you." He slid two fingers into her this time, spreading her open, willing her muscles to relax. She writhed beneath him, and he had to hold her hip to keep her from hurting herself.

"Spread your legs a little more," he ordered. When she complied, his entire body shot out of control. He could see everything. Her heart-shaped ass, the pink pucker of her anus and her wet, swollen cunt. She was completely on display.

"It feels forbidden, doesn't it?" he asked. She replied with a jerky nod as she buried her face into the bedspread. "You've always been my forbidden pleasure, Gracie. Each time I looked at you, I knew I had no business thinking what I was thinking. You were too young, too innocent. But it never seemed to matter, because I still wanted you."

She lifted her head and started to speak, but he slid his fingers in another inch and all that came out was a whimper. Jackson was buried clear to his knuckles inside Grace's ass.

"There are a lot of sensitive nerve endings around your anus. When my cock fills you, it's going to feel so damn good. Spreading you open and pumping into you. Tell me. Admit you want me there. Give me permission, baby."

"Yes, Jackson."

Just what he wanted to hear. "You will be able to feel every throb." He leaned over her and whispered into her ear. "Every inch will feel like another taste of paradise. Then, when I come, you'll feel the heat of it shooting through you. Would you like me to come inside of you? Right here—" he wiggled his fingers for emphasis "—in this tight little ass where no man has ever touched?"

"You make me want things. I've never felt so ready to come and you've not even touched my clit. Please don't make me wait."

Her passion equaled his, but he couldn't take her, not just

yet. "I want to make sure you're ready for me." He pulled his fingers free and added a third, then thrust inside, stretching her, pushing her beyond her comfort zone. He made every attempt to go slow, allowing her body to adjust to the invasion. She moaned and spread her legs further, pressed backward against his hand, as if anxious for more.

"Mmm, that's it, pet," he murmured. "Now you're ready." Jackson's body was on fire and his dick ached for release. He couldn't wait another second.

He reached for the bottle of lotion once more and poured a small amount over his aching cock, already swollen and dripping with pre-come at the thought of being buried deep. Gently, Jackson separated the round globes of Grace's backside and touched the head of his cock to her entrance. Alert to any sign of pain, he pushed the head of cock inside. It was such sweet torture to hold back from thrusting deeply. His body was desperate to fuck her hard and fast.

She cried out his name and clutched the bedspread above her head. As he slipped in another inch, she thrust backward.

He held her hips in place. "Easy, baby. Let me take you there slowly."

Another inch more and she tried to take control of their lovemaking by pushing herself onto him. He bit back a curse as the action caused his cock to slip in another inch. "Slow down or you'll hurt yourself," he commanded.

She was new to this type of sexual pleasure and didn't understand that they couldn't rush this first time. He refused to cause her even an ounce of pain—despite the way his primal instincts kept battering at him to fill her.

As he held her down, Jackson heard Grace let loose a needy little whimper. The yearning, delicate sound turned his heart to mush and he gave her another thick inch of his hard flesh. In the same instant, he took his right hand from her hip and toyed with the tempting little bud of her clitoris. He watched her back arch, her hands clutching the bedspread as she became a slave to her body's delicious sensations. With no warning she screamed his name and pushed against him as her orgasm took her. It was sheer ecstasy to bring her to all new heights of pleasure.

"Now," he snarled. "All of me."

"Yes!"

A rumbling growl escaped him at her feral response. He pushed himself the rest of the way inside her tightest opening, her muscles sucked him in and she immediately tensed.

Jackson swore, then swore again. The pleasure-pain of her body's clutch was the best sort of torment.

"Fuck, ease up, Grace."

"I-I can't," she cried.

Jackson reached up and stroked her sweat soaked hair away from her face, then covered her body with his larger frame, folding himself around her protectively. He kissed her upturned cheek and felt her inner muscles relax. He thanked the heavens above. Much more of her clenching and he would have embarrassed himself.

"Good girl." He bit the smooth line of her neck, pleased when she all but purred for him. He licked and suckled at her neck, knowing now how much she liked it, and began a gentle rhythm with his hips. Leisurely he built the pace until his overheated flesh was slapping against hers.

"You belong to me."

She didn't speak, only licked her lips and pushed against him, joining in the rhythm of their beautiful dance. Soon he felt himself swell and his balls drew up tight. One more thrust and he was there, his cock erupting inside her, hot fluid filling her. She shouted his name and joined him with her own climactic finish.

Jackson kissed Grace's cheek, then her neck. "You make me lose control."

"I know what you mean."

Jackson slipped his cock free of her tight opening, then sat back on his knees and stared down at the little blonde beauty who'd stolen his heart with a few sarcastic comments. It was unbelievable he'd gone his entire life keeping his heart safe, only to have it snatched away by a woman too sassy for her good. He moved off the bed and said, "Come on, shower time."

"I can't move, but you go ahead."

He shook his head, then swatted her ass. She jerked and glared at him. "What was that for?"

He held out his hand. "Get your cute ass in gear. We need a shower, then we need to see about the conference."

She muttered to herself and scooted across the bed. "I suppose I should spend at least a little time looking over the different software companies. Vaughn is due for some upgrades."

Jackson grabbed her as she started around him toward the bathroom. He pulled her in tight and took her mouth in a demanding mating of lips. As he felt her surrender, he dipped low, swung her into his arms and carried her to the bathroom. He licked at the seam of her lips before lifting his head. He looked at the huge tub and changed his mind about a quick shower. Leaving Grace standing in the middle of the room nibbling at her lower lip, Jackson turned on the faucets and adjusted the temperature of the water until it was just right.

"I thought you wanted to shower?"

He held out a hand and she took it willingly, a shy smile crossing her face. "Changed my mind." He let her step in first, before he moved in behind her and sat down. She settled between his legs before he grabbed the soap and washcloth.

"No bubble bath?"

He smoothed the cloth over her slick skin and felt his cock begin to stir. "It'd only detract from the view."

Grace was silent as he started to clean her. He made his way down over her torso, then massaged the washcloth between her thighs. It wasn't long before the washcloth became annoying. He dropped it in the water and let his fingers journey over Grace's smooth skin. When he moved upward, touching the plump flesh of her breasts, she quivered. He imagined what it might be like to have her this way every morning, soft, trusting, ready for his pleasure.

"You're so pretty, baby," Jackson murmured. "I love the way you react to my touch." He pinched her nipple and Grace arched forward. "You make me lose my mind."

"I love your touch," Grace breathed out. She lifted her arm and clutched his forearm, as if afraid he'd disappear if she let go. He could've told her he wasn't about to go anywhere.

Jackson's skimmed his fingers back and forth over each puffy nipple, forcing them to tight peaks. He inched his way over her ribcage to her hips, before cupping her mound. "Mmm, my pretty little baby," he whispered against her ear. "So soft and sweet."

Grace spread her legs wider, giving him the advantage. He dipped his finger into her pussy, pulling another moan from her. He was slow and gentle, the need to savor each touch paramount in his mind. There would be no speeding to the finish line this time. He used his other hand to pinch her clitoris between his finger and thumb, rolling and squeezing the

215

tight bundle of nerves. His blood ran hot as her pussy clenched around him.

"Oh, God, I want you," she admitted. "I feel like I've wanted you forever."

"Me too, sweetheart, but let me make love to you for a bit. There's no hurry."

He emphasized his words by letting another finger join the first inside her wet heat. His cock pressed against her bottom and he had to force back the need to plunge it deep inside her hot little ass. Grace pushed her lower body into his hand, working herself into a frenzy.

He kissed her neck and sucked at her pulse, giving her a small purple mark. "Mine," he growled.

"Please," Grace begged, her voice hoarse from her earlier shouts.

He placed a series of soft kisses down her shoulder and hummed against her wet skin, "You're so sexy like this, baby. All slick and eager. I could drown in you." Smoothing his fingers over Grace's fleshy labia, he watched as she flung her head back and moaned deep, pushing against his hand. Her desperation fueled his hunger.

Moving his fingers inside her quicker, he found just the right rhythm, caressing her into a wild fervor. When she was nearly there, he pulled all the way out, then plunged deep. He pumped himself against the supple flesh of her ass while he finger-fucked her tight pussy, helpless to stop the firestorm raging inside him. Without warning Grace burst apart, her inner muscles holding his fingers tightly. Her bucking body pushed him over the edge and had him coming in hot spurts against her body, coating them both with his seed.

Jackson wrapped his other arm around her middle as her orgasm continued, holding her snug against him. After they both caught their breath, he cupped her face and forced to look at him. "No woman has ever made me lose control so easily." He pressed his lips to hers, soft and easy, before coaxing her lips open. When she sighed and let him in, he sucked at her tongue, dying for a taste of her, aching to make the moment last forever. Slowly, he lifted his lips from hers.

She let out a shaky breath, then said, "I have no control with you. You speak and I melt. You smile and butterflies fill my stomach. You steal a woman's sanity and it's really not fair."

He grinned down at her. "Then we're on equal ground here, *pet*, because it's the same for me."

Neither of them said another word. They simply lingered in the tub until the water turned cold, enjoying the moment. As they toweled off, Jackson waited for Grace to say something, anything, about her feelings. To give him at least a hint at what she felt for him. As she started to dress for the conference, his frustration won out. He snatched her blouse out of her hand and held it above her head. "Whoa, that's it? You don't have anything to say?"

Her brows shot upward. "What do you mean?"

"Don't play with me," he gritted out. "You know what I'm talking about. We just shared something incredible and you're going to go into work mode without a backward glance?"

She pushed her hair behind her ear. "I loved what we did, you know that. It was wonderful, but I don't know what more you want from me."

Jackson took her chin in his palm and forced her to meet his gaze. "I want a relationship with you. I want to belong to you and I want you to belong to me. I won't accept anything less."

She placed her hand against his cheek, her expression one of concern. "I'm not sure it's smart, but I think I'm falling for you." He started to lay his own feelings on the line, but she placed two fingers against his lips, forestalling any declarations of love everlasting.

"You should know that I didn't want to care about you. I tried really hard not to, in fact. You aren't the type to settle down. I've seen you with other women. You don't stay with a woman for more than a few months. I'm not interested in being dumped once the newness wears off. If you can't offer me more than a short term sexfest, then we end things now and be glad for what we had." She took a deep breath and went on. "After the car accident, when I was told I'd have a hard time bringing a baby to full term, I sort of convinced myself I didn't have much to offer a man. I'm still uncertain. There are a lot of *ifs* involved there, but I do know that I'm tired of worrying about what may never be."

Jackson took her head in the palms of his hands. "First of all, if we have kids, great. If not, that's okay too. Giving birth doesn't make you more of a woman in my estimation. Second, I've not had a serious relationship because the only woman who could ever fill that spot is standing in front of me. I've watched you for over a year. We've been driving each other crazy dancing around the issue, but the truth is, I don't think either of us was ready. I love you, Gracie. You and only you. I'm too damned old for you, and you deserve someone who can be sweet and gentle, but I won't give you up. This isn't a sexfest. Although that does sound intriguing." She elbowed him in the ribs, and he chuckled. "Seriously, baby, this is the real deal."

Jackson was horrified when Grace's soft blue eyes welled up. He'd rather lie on a bed of nails than watch Grace cry. "This is the real deal for me too," she admitted shyly.

He swiped at a tear that trickled down her cheek and whispered, "Good. Now, let's get this damned conference out of the way so we can get back here and play with that rope a little more."

Her cheeks turned pink. "You want to bind me again?"

Jackson reached around and smacked her ass, causing her to yelp, before handing her blouse back to her. "There's twenty-five feet of rope there, pet, I can do a lot of tying with that much."

She went up on her toes and whispered, "You are so depraved."

Their lips touched, and suddenly the conference was forgotten again.

Epilogue

Three weeks later...

"Merrick, I'm not turning in my expenses, and if you suggest it one more time, I'm going to blow a gasket. I didn't do a lick of work the entire time I was in Vegas. It was more or less a vacation."

Grace was getting good and tired of having this conversation. From the time they'd arrived back in Ohio, Merrick had been all questions. When she'd finally relented and told him that Jackson and she were now an item, he'd started threatening Jackson to within an inch of his life if he so much as made her sad. Now he wouldn't let up about reimbursing her for the Vegas trip.

"You aren't taking advantage of me if I want to pay for the damned trip, so turn in your expenses."

"She won't change her mind, trust me. I should know."

Grace pivoted on her heel to find Jackson lounging against Merrick's office door, a devilish grin on his handsome face. His tan pants and black polo shirt showed off his muscular body. Her mouth watered as she remembered how they'd started out the day. She'd woken in Jackson's bed, his mouth between her thighs. She'd reciprocated, of course.

"Earth to Grace."

She turned at the sound of her cousin's annoyed voice. "What?"

Merrick waved her out of his office. "Go, it's no use trying to talk to you when you have that glazed-over look in your eyes."

Jackson stepped forward and wrapped an arm around her waist. "Ready to go home?"

She nodded. "I just need to grab my purse. I'll meet you by the elevators." She started to move away, but he was faster. His head descended, their lips met. It was too brief, and Grace badly needed more. "Tease," she muttered as she stalked from the office, his chuckle trailing after her.

As she approached her desk, one of the other female employees came up to her. Marty was it? No, Marly. She'd never cared much for the other woman. Her catty gossiping in the break room had grated on her nerves more than once.

"So, you and Jackson have been pretty hot and heavy for...what? Three weeks now?"

Grace had no idea where this conversation was leading, but knowing Marly, it wasn't going to make her happy. "Uh, yeah, I guess." Grace took her purse off the back of her chair and turned toward the woman.

"So, that means you have about a week left before he boots you out of his bed."

Ah, here it came. Envy, and it was never pretty. "You think?"

The woman looked down her nose at her. Grace had never actually seen someone physically do that, but Marly was quite capable, considering she was six-foot-three. "He never keeps a woman longer than a month," she sneered. "Hope you didn't give up your apartment. You'll probably need it again soon, hun."

Grace stepped forward and gave her anger free rein. "Be very careful what you say about Jackson. I don't much care for people who trash my family."

Marly stepped back. "He's not even close to being your family."

Grace stepped forward again, noting the way Marly paled. "He's mine, remember that. I protect my own."

"No need to get nasty. I'm just giving you a friendly warning. It's no skin off my nose if you don't heed it."

She stomped off, leaving Grace in a predicament. She could clock the bitch, but then that wouldn't be very professional. Or she could do the adult thing and let it go.

"She's not worth it, baby."

The deep baritone behind her had her pussy throbbing. She turned to find Jackson standing several feet away, his hands in his pockets. She couldn't read his expression. Had he heard the woman's caustic remarks? "She deserved a black eye for what she said about you."

Jackson closed the distance separating them and took her in his arms. "I love you, Gracie. I'm not getting tired of you. Give me about fifty years and maybe that'll change, but I highly doubt it will even then."

"And I love you," she said on a sigh as she wrapped her arms around his neck. "Now, let's go home. It's my turn with the rope."

"Uh, baby, I thought we talked about that."

Grace let her hand travel down his back to cup his ass. "Chicken?"

His grin lit her on fire. "Bring it on, *pet.*"

About the Author

To learn more about Anne Rainey, please visit http://annerainey.com. Send an email to Anne at anne@annerainey.com or join her Yahoo! group to join in the fun with other readers as well as Anne! http://groups.yahoo.com/group/rb_afterdark

Breinigsville, PA USA
27 May 2010
238839BV00001B/19/P